OBSIDIAN FAITH

BEV ELLE

Obsidian Faith

Editing by Rare Bird Editing www.rarebirdediting.com

Book design by Thaigher Lillian

This book is a work of fiction. The names, characters, places and incidents are products of the writer's imagination or have been used fictitiously and are not to be construed as real. Any resemblance to persons, living or dead, actual events, locale or organizations is entirely coincidental.

Printed in the USA by Divine Nine, LLC via Bev Elle Press 2014
CreateSpace Trade Paperback Edition

ISBN 978-0-9905062-2-5

First Edition: December 2014

14 13 12 11 10 / 10 9 8 7 6 5 4 3 2 1

Table of Contents

Bev Elle's Newsletter Sign-up Form: http://eepurl.com/3PosH

PART ONE: The Substance of Things Hoped For

Chapter One

February 1997

"Leave me alone!"

The plaintive wail got to him. At ten, Trevor Landon knew to mind his own business, but something about the little girl, Shanice, the newest resident at the Baptist children's home, made him feel protective. Trevor had learned in his short three years in the system to keep his head down. He was only an orphan, after all. Not an idiot. Sometimes orphans had to be selfish in order to survive, but today he couldn't ignore the cruelty, even though it wasn't directed at him.

Maybe his reaction to Shanice was because she reminded him of his little sister, Natalie, who'd been about her age when their crazy-assed mom decided child-rearing wasn't for her. A few weeks shy of her fourth birthday, and his seventh, Natalie stepped into an open elevator shaft while dear old mom was taking them on a field trip at three a.m. to score some meth from her local dealer.

That was the last straw for the Department of Children and Family Services, and they inducted Trevor into the foster care system. When his mother overdosed six months later, he became a "permanent resident of the system." His mother may not have killed his sister with her own hands, but she might as well have. He didn't know what the hell had saved *his* life, and he had mixed feelings about it most of the time. That was about to change.

"Stop it!" Shanice said.

She had a cute little voice with the slightest lisp. He moved away from the computer, which is where he planted himself most days after his chores were done.

A couple of older children were picking on her, and he'd had enough. Trevor wasn't a vigilante, per se, but he'd certainly learned to take care of himself since he'd become a ward of the church-operated facility.

"Give it back," Shanice said, now near tears. She reached in vain for the teddy bear the bullies had taken from her. One boy, Darrien, and a girl, Shayla, both taller and bigger, were playing keep-away with it.

"Don't be such a baby." Shayla sneered. "There's no room for teddy bears in a children's home." She tossed the bear to her partner as Shanice looked on in terror.

"Yeah, a baby in diapers even," Darrien said. "They only adopt babies from this joint, so maybe you're onto something." He tossed the bear back to Shayla.

Shanice reached for her toy. "I don't care. Give it. It's mine."

Trevor stepped up to Darrien, who he bested in height by an inch or so. "Give the little girl her toy back. Now," he said, careful to make his ten-year-old voice sound as ominous as he could.

"What's it to ya?" Shayla asked. "This brat your little sister, or something?"

Hitting a girl, no matter how mean, wasn't an option, but he remembered what his mom used to do. A few well-placed pinches and she dropped the teddy bear, which Shanice promptly scooped up. When Darrien moved into Trevor's personal space, fists raised, Trevor tagged him with a perfect right hook. Blood spewed from the boy's nose like a geyser, and he cried harder than Shanice had just moments ago.

With all the noise they made, they wound up in the office of the house parents, an apprentice pastor named Isaiah Bailey, and his wife, Brenda. Trevor liked them better than the last house parents, because they were fair and actually listened to what the kids had to say. Isaiah had a pro wrestler's build, but he was a kind man. While Brenda took care of Darrien, Isaiah took them, one-by-one, out into the common area to get their stories.

Afterward, Isaiah said, "I have two of you telling one version of events and two telling me another. It's almost dinner time and I want to get to the bottom of this. Right now, Trevor, I can say you're clearly the aggressor, because you pinched Shayla and punched Darrien."

"They were asking for it. Picking on Shanice who's new and younger than the both of 'em."

Isaiah touched Trevor's shoulder in a calming gesture. "That may be true, son, but how do we handle conflict here?"

"With our words, not our fists," Trevor mumbled.

"Now, how am I to rule on this one? Shayla and Darrien say you used violence against them for no reason. They were just playing with Shanice."

"What if I can prove them wrong?" Trevor said.

"How would you do that?"

"I left the video cam running on the PC when I asked them to stop bothering Shanice."

Isaiah's eyebrows rose. "Want to play the video back for me?"

"Sure."

Pastor Bailey was so impressed with Trevor's video surveillance he began to use the makeshift security cams to help figure out who was breaking the rules and to solve disputes. Trevor was able to do things on the PC the average adult couldn't do. This included writing programs and retrofitting the outdated systems.

Recognizing Trevor's skill, Pastor Bailey introduced Trevor to his friend David Kyle, a Harvard-educated computer programmer who'd also been a Marine intelligence officer. David was one of the best "white hat hackers" in the world, and he began grooming Trevor when he was able to get up to the Sanford facility. But the majority of their mentoring sessions were done by computer.

After the incident with the bullies, two things changed. Because of David Kyle, Trevor's computer skills improved exponentially, and Shanice was so thankful for his help, she became his lifelong fan club of one. She was never far from him when they got home from school, and she always sat next to him at dinner. They fell into a routine of doing their homework together in the common room. Shanice would try to get Trevor, who usually liked to keep to himself, to talk to her any way she could.

"Can you write all your letters and numbers?" Shanice asked.

"Yeah," he said. "You kinda have to know that stuff in order to do homework."

"My homework *is* writing letters and numbers...and making colors," she said glumly. "When will I be able to write lots of stuff like you?"

"Probably when you're about second grade," he said.

"Good, because I'm bored."

She colored another picture, being careful to stay inside the lines, while Trevor turned back to his own math homework. She stopped coloring and sighed.

"Trevor, do you remember your Mommy?"

He frowned. "Yeah, probably more than I would like to. How about you?"

"Yeah. She got sick and throwed up then went to sleep and didn't wake back up. The lady in the blue suit brought me here, and I didn't see her again."

"What about your Dad?"

"I never had a daddy. Mommy had lots of boyfriends, though."

"Don't tell that to the other kids. Darrien and Shayla will use it against you." Trevor learned this the hard way when he naively believed all the other kids in the home were his friends.

"Okay. It can be our secret."

Trevor also knew about mothers who sold their bodies for money and drugs. He didn't like to think about how he'd never know his dad, because it hurt. Even though Shanice was half his age, he knew he could trust her. It was likely neither he nor Shanice would ever know their biological fathers.

"I miss my Mommy. Do you miss yours?" she asked. Her brown eyes were wide with curiosity.

"I do, and I don't." Trevor missed the mom he'd never known. The one before she became a meth-head.

"I have a picture of my Mommy. You want to see it?" Shanice asked.

"Yeah, sure."

She picked up the tiny locket she wore around her neck all the time and opened it. Inside was a picture of a brown-skinned African American woman who looked to be in her early twenties, and on the other side was a white baby.

"This is my Mommy before I was born, and this is a picture of me when I was a baby."

Trevor pushed his blonde hair out of his eyes and studied the pictures.

"Uh... nice." He didn't have many good family memories, so he didn't quite know what to say.

"You know what we should do, Trevor?"

"What?"

"We should adopt each other, since we don't have a Mommy or Daddy."

"Okay." He grinned. "We can be like the two musketeers."

Shanice looked confused. "What's a musketeer?"

"They were like these special soldiers who guarded the king of France a long time ago. Their special motto, uh, saying, was 'one for all and all for one.'"

She looked more confused. "And what does that mean?"

"They had each other's back... looked out for each other."

"Like we're always going to do, right?" She said and gave him a big smile.

"Right."

From that day forward, in Shanice's eyes, Trevor could do no wrong.

Chapter Two

Trevor and Shanice were in the common room a few months later, when Brenda Bailey came to them. Trevor was manipulating a screen of computer code, and Shanice was sitting in a comfy chair not far from him reading a book. She smiled at them. Brenda loved how he and Shanice had bonded and had told Trevor as much, but he knew her too well. She was about to give them some news he wasn't going to like.

"Thought I'd find you two out here," Brenda said.

Trevor and Shanice gave her their undivided attention.

"Hey, Ms. Brenda," they said almost in unison.

"Would you two come to the office? Isaiah and I have some news for you."

Trevor was sure it wasn't to tell him he was adopted. The older he got, the less likely it was to happen. Shanice stood a greater chance, because she was adorable and still young enough to luck out. But he wasn't sure how he would feel if that happened for her. She'd taken Natalie's place, and there wasn't anything he wouldn't do for her.

When they entered Pastor Isaiah's office, David Kyle and another woman were there.

"Trevor, Shanice, you know David Kyle, and this is David's wife, Elena."

Elena Kyle looked happy to meet them. But even though the Baileys were cool, after what his mom did, Trevor still didn't trust adults until they'd earned it.

Isaiah smiled and said, "In a couple of weeks, Brenda and I are leaving the home, because I'm accepting the pastorate at Trinity Baptist Church in Orlando, but we've begun proceedings to adopt Shanice, so she'll be going with us."

Shanice ran to Brenda, who had her arms waiting to receive the new addition to their family.

"Oh, Ms. Brenda," Shanice said. "You're going to be my mommy!"

"Yes, I am," Brenda said.

Then she stood back and said. "Are you and Pastor Isaiah going to be Trevor's mommy and daddy, too?"

The question caught them briefly off guard. Then Pastor Isaiah finished the rest of his news. "Trevor is going to be adopted by Mr. and Mrs. Kyle."

To say Trevor was stunned was an understatement. The Kyles seemed like decent folks, especially David, but Trevor would reserve judgment until he got a chance to know them better as his foster parents.

"But I don't want to leave Trevor," Shanice said, her bottom lip trembled, as her eyes filled with tears.

Brenda kneeled in front of Shanice so they were on eye level. "You won't have to. Not really. The Kyles live in Orlando right down the street from where we'll be living. You'll see Trevor all the time."

Trevor tried not to smile. To stay cool. But he couldn't. He felt his face break into a grin. The best he could do was to dial his smile a little lower than Shanice's.

·········●··········

Getting a new family was a dream come true for Trevor. All he'd ever wanted was someone to care about him, to truly care what happened to him. To love him.

When Trevor entered the two-story Tudor house with the red brick, white trim, and red shutters, he finally felt as if he was home. When the Kyles wrapped him in their arms, he knew it was what he'd been waiting for all his life. He grabbed his duffle bag and unpacked it in what would be the first room he'd had to himself, ever. Then he went to explore the rest of the property. There was a huge backyard with a screen-covered pool and the greenest grass he'd ever seen. He couldn't wait to play catch with David, as if he were a regular kid.

Like any other kid in a place that was almost perpetually sunny, Trevor played sports. Oddly, he found he was good at them, despite being the biggest geek alive. Growing up in Orlando was the best. It was an orphan child's wildest dream. Disneyworld was practically in his backyard, and there was never a lack for anything to do.

As time went on, Trevor realized the Kyles were almost as nice as Pastor Isaiah and Brenda. Sure, they had to get through some rough parts, mostly because of his trust issues, and the Kyles had to set him straight about what they expected from him. Even though David was a former marine, he was as much a computer geek as Trevor. And Elena was kind of a pushover.

Trevor settled into a routine that resembled family life for the first time. Just as the Baileys promised, if he wasn't at their house, Shanice was at the Kyles. He and Shanice got to play and swim together with the other neighborhood kids, to go to Trevor's games with the Kyles, and to Shanice's dance recitals and other activities. The summer flew by, and he and Shanice were enrolled in a school affiliated with Pastor Isaiah's church, rather than Orange County public schools, so this meant they were able to go to the same school for a change. Brenda and Elena took turns driving them.

The night before the first day of school, David came into Trevor's room to talk to him. He was already in his pajamas and about to go to sleep.

"Ready for your big day tomorrow, son?"

"Yes, sir." Trevor said. He'd learned David appreciated the title of respect, because he'd been in the Corps for so long.

David reached into his wallet and pulled out a twenty. "Here's lunch money and pocket change. Elena will set up an account once you bring home all your paperwork, so you won't have to carry cash."

"Thanks." Trevor took the twenty and put it in the nylon wallet Elena had purchased for him with all his other back-to-school stuff. Small gestures like that made him happy but still afraid he somehow didn't deserve it. He tried never to take anything for granted.

David fidgeted with the parts of a model car they were working on together. Trevor could tell he wanted to speak to him about something else. Finally, he turned around and straddled the desk chair facing Trevor, who yawned widely.

"You're tired, so I'll say this and let you get to sleep."

"Okay, sir." Trevor sat up so he could pay better attention.

"You have unique skills in math and computer science that surpass those of many men I've known in the field. You have a God-given talent for it, and some day you will be able to hold your own among the best in the world." David smiled, and Trevor could see the pride in his eyes. It made him get a lump in his throat, but he tried not to show his emotion.

"I love working on computers more than anything. Thank you so much for letting me have one in my room."

"You're welcome," David said, then he seemed to think about it. "As long as you don't abuse the privilege."

"I won't. I promise." Trevor said, trying to sound as sincere as he could.

"I'd like you to not call any attention to yourself by showing off at school. Elena and I are doing this to protect you, because if some academics or branches of the government learned of your abilities, they might exploit you in ways you're not ready for. Do you understand, Trevor?"

"You mean they might try to study me like they'd do if they ever discovered an alien on the planet?"

"Yeah, like that and worse. They could likely label you as a threat to every computer system in the world and stop you from practicing what you love."

That frightened him. "I won't be a show-off, Mr. Kyle, I promise." He still wasn't ready to call them "Mom" and "Dad" yet, but he wanted to someday, just like Shanice already did with the Baileys

"Oh, I want you to do well and to get good grades, but don't go above and beyond what they're teaching in your grade level. We'll do the extra-curriculars at home."

"Okay, I'll remember."

David stood and put the chair back under the desk. Then he turned as if he remembered something. "I'm sure this goes without saying, but don't forget to watch out for Shanice. You're the only big brother she's ever known and first grade can be scary."

"I'll make sure no one picks on her," Trevor said.

"Don't try to handle it yourself, though. Report it to a school official. I won't have you fighting at school."

Trevor felt every bit like the protective big brother where Shanice was concerned, but he knew he couldn't disappoint David. "Oh, all right."

David looked like he was trying to keep himself from laughing as he turned to leave. "Goodnight, Trevor."

"Goodnight, sir."

Chapter Three

At school, Shanice would sometimes ask Trevor to do embarrassing things. Like asking him to carry her *Hello Kitty* backpack when her arms were full, or loaning her lunch money when she bought extra stuff and used up all the money in her account before she should have, and the worse, having him talk to her teddy like he was human sometimes.

Trevor never denied her when it was something he could do. When she got it into her head that she wanted to join in an activity at school, she came to Trevor at the end of the day and asked for his help. He was waiting in the car pickup area when she joined him later than usual with a flyer in her hand.

"What you got there, 'Nice?" Sometimes he shortened her name when he was lazy.

"It's a flyer about the Fall Festival. And guess what?"

He laughed. When she got excited about something, she got everyone excited about it. "What?"

"I'm going to sing in the talent show."

He folded his arms. "Yeah?"

OBSIDIAN FAITH • 14

"Yeah."

"And what're you going to sing?"

"This Little Light of Mine." She'd been singing in the children's choir at Pastor Isaiah's church, and that song was by far her favorite. Then she said, "And you're going to play the music for me, like you do at church."

Trevor did work the sound board on Sundays with David. Then he remembered how David said he didn't want Trevor to call attention to himself, so he didn't know whether he should agree.

"I don't know. I'll have to ask David and Elena about it."

"They won't mind," Shanice said. She had become such a confident little person. The Baileys had done that.

Of course, when Trevor asked David about the talent show, David not only said Trevor could do it, he introduced him to the *Garage Band* application, and Trevor used it to accompany his surrogate sister during her singing debut at the Fall Festival. Trevor dared any of his friends to give him any grief about it.

· · · · · · · · ● · · · · · · · · · ·

The Kyles and Baileys had a huge block party when their adoptions of Trevor and Shanice went through. The cul-de-sac where the Baileys resided was chock full of people, and Isaiah, being a sucker for a captive audience, took a few moments to say a few words.

"As many of you know, the position I held prior to taking on my role at Trinity was as a house parent at a Baptist Children's facility. During our stint there, Brenda and I had the honor and privilege of taking care of some wonderful, and some not-so-wonderful children." The crowd laughed. "However, we loved them all and did everything we could to prepare them for whatever fate the Lord had in store for them. While there, David and I fell in love with the two most amazing children known to man: our daughter, Shanice, and the Kyles' son, Trevor."

"What are Elena and I, liverwurst?" Brenda yelled.

"I'm getting to that part, sweetheart," Isaiah said. Then he beckoned to Trevor and Shanice, who joined hands and walked over to their adoptive parents. "Trevor was this serious little guy who always had his nose in the dilapidated old computer, and Shanice was this breath of fresh air who charmed everyone. Brenda got the ball rolling when she came to bed one night and confessed she had a favorite among the children. Shanice had wormed her way into Brenda's heart, and she got it into her head that she was now unfit to be a house parent because she wasn't objective anymore." Brenda glared playfully at him, and he continued. "After I counseled my wife and talked her out of stepping down from our posts immediately, we discussed the prospect of adopting. Of course, knowing how close Shanice was to Trevor, we realized we simply couldn't take her and leave him there. David was already mentoring Trevor, so it only took a suggestion from me to get him to take his plea to Elena. And the rest, as they say is history."

He then called the wives over. "Brenda, Elena, come share with our friends what you have in your hands."

Brenda grabbed the mike and held up the legal document. "Elena and I have in our hands the adoption decrees and pristine birth certificates of our children. Isaiah and I are the proud parents of Shanice Anderson Bailey."

Elena said, "And David and I are the proud parents of Trevor Landon Kyle." Their adoptive parents had decided to use their original names as their middle names, so they would always remember their origins, just in case sometime in the future they wanted to find some of the members of their families.

The crowd cheered as the Baileys and Kyles shared hugs with each other, and then their friends and family.

Trevor and Shanice were formally introduced to all the neighbors and the extended families of the Baileys and Kyles. He also met David's younger brother, Philip. Trevor noticed he looked sleazy, and had his arm around a woman who had almost nothing on and too much makeup. He could also tell Philip didn't like children, even though he gave Trevor and Shanice a bunch of gifts.

"Trevor this is my brother, Philip. Your uncle."

"Hey, Trevor," Philip said. "Try not to become the black sheep of the family like me, eh?"

"Phil..." David shook his head. "He's only eleven."

"It's all right, sir," Trevor said. "I was the only sheep left in my family until now."

Shanice grabbed Trevor's hand. "C'mon Trevor, let's dance." Brenda had put Shanice in a dance class and dancing was all she wanted to do at the time.

Trevor didn't consider himself any good at dancing, but Shanice seemed happy with his moves, so he didn't mind making a fool of himself. For the next four years, they had the best family lives any kid could ask for, and despite their age difference they remained close.

Chapter Four

April 2001

"Mom and Dad are late," Trevor said. It still sounded weird to call them that sometimes, even though it was almost the fourth anniversary of his adoption. "They said they'd be back in time for dinner."

He eyed the steaming hot dishes on display before him on the Baileys dinner table. His stomach growled an audible displeasure for denying his almost fifteen-year-old digestive system the sustenance it craved. Trevor looked at the clock. David and Elena were already a half an hour later coming back from the church-sponsored marriage retreat than he'd anticipated, and denying himself Brenda's delicious cooking was a special form of torture.

Brenda gestured toward the unused place setting Trevor occupied next to Shanice where he had yet to dish out any food. "You could eat just a little bit and save a fraction of your stomach for whatever Elena's going to prepare later."

"You know Mom's macaroni and cheese is better than anything in the box," Shanice said, holding a forkful just under his nose to tempt him even further. Trevor gobbled up the pasta so quickly he took the fork from her hand.

Shanice giggled. "Give me my fork back." Trevor pulled the tines slowly between his lips, making sure he got ever bit of the gooey cheese off the fork. Shanice then pulled a face, "On second thought, keep that fork. I'll take your unused one." She grabbed Trevor's fork before he could protest.

Isaiah took another helping and passed Trevor the crock. "Might as well eat something for now. A growing young man like you'll be hungry again in a couple of hours anyway."

"Okay," Trevor said, and took the dish and ladled out a generous helping of macaroni and cheese onto his plate, plus a little bit of the other entrees as well.

After dinner, Trevor, Isaiah, Shanice, and Tanya, the Baileys' current foster child, played a game of horse on the carport in front of the house, while Brenda, who'd just given birth to twins took advantage of napping while the babies were down. They were arguing over whether or not Shanice had been over the line when she made her most recent point when an Orange County Sheriff's vehicle pulled up in front of the house.

Isaiah lobbed the ball to Trevor. "Keep playing, and make sure Shanice doesn't cheat. I'll be right back."

Trevor wanted to keep playing. He also didn't want to think about what the Sheriff's car showing up now that David and Elena were almost two hours late meant. Isaiah's grief-stricken look after one of the deputies spoke to him was enough to clue Trevor in that something was terribly wrong, and even though he wanted to scream and run away from whatever news they were bringing, he was rooted to the spot.

Trevor took his turn and then another, and then another, arcing perfect shot, after perfect shot into the goal as the Sheriff's deputies pulled away and Isaiah came back to join them.

"Dad, Trevor's cheating," Shanice complained.

"It's okay, honey," Isaiah said. "Why don't you and Tanya go get some ice cream while I have a talk with Trevor."

"Okay," Shanice said, obedient although her forehead was wrinkled in confusion.

The girls were barely at the door when Trevor stopped shooting the ball and turned to Isaiah. "They're not coming back, are they?" he said, outwardly calm, but enraged inside.

Isaiah reached for him, enfolding Trevor in his arms as the ball dropped at their feet. "No, son. I'm sorry."

When Trevor was able to pull himself together enough not to bawl like a baby, he asked "What happened?"

"Law enforcement is still investigating, but their car went off the road into some trees not far from Ocoee. They died on impact. Another car was involved, but when the Sheriff arrived no one else was on scene."

"What kind of person does that?" Trevor said, but what he was thinking was, *I'm an orphan again.* His parents had been almost home when someone selfishly took them away from him. Trevor felt worse at twice the age he'd been when he first went into the system, if that were possible.

· · · · · · · · ·●· · · · · · · · · ·

Everyone in the Bailey household were in bed, including Trevor. He again occupied the guest room while Shanice and Tanya doubled up, but he was unable to sleep. All he could think of was David and Elena, and how they would never scold him again about leaving his socks all over the place, or about brushing his teeth even after snacks.

He would miss David writing programs with him, and Elena making her famous Italian dishes, and both of them going to his sports games and school events as his parents. Most of all, he would miss their hugs, which he'd tolerated when he first came to live with them, but had grown to expect and require, about as much as he needed air to breathe.

Since he'd heard the news, the pain of their loss had lodged in his heart and would not budge. He felt as if he were suffocating from it, because nothing and no one could bring them back. Trevor turned, punched the pillow, and settled in another position.

He was watching the red LED numbers on the clock count forward in time when he heard the door open, then the footprints of a small person walking toward the bed. He didn't have to turn around to see who it was.

"Trevor? Are you asleep?" Shanice stage-whispered.

"No," he said.

That was apparently all the invitation she needed. Shanice went around to the other side and hopped into bed with him.

"It's way past your bedtime. You're going to be in so much trouble," he said.

"Not if you don't tell on me," she said, and snuggled under the cover next to him. They lay side by side in silence for a while until Shanice couldn't stand it. "Mom and Dad won't let them take you away again, Trevor. You'll see."

Her confidence was reassuring. He'd been hurting so much for David and Elena he hadn't thought of where he would go if they hadn't made some arrangements for him. His uncle Philip had called Isaiah promising to contact them again with the funeral plans, and asking if Trevor wanted to come stay with him, but Isaiah had thankfully declined.

"I asked Dad if Uncle David and Aunt Elena were in heaven and he said they were," Shanice said with the certainty of a ten-year-old whose budding faith could not be shaken.

"You know what I think?"

"What?" she said.

"I think it sucks that they're gone. It sucks that whoever hit their car didn't even stop to see if they were okay, or to call the police. And it really sucks that I'm never going to see them again!"

Shanice didn't call him on getting so loud that he could've woken up the whole house. She just scooted closer and hugged his neck. Trevor was so overcome by her offer of comfort his heart unclenched and all the pain lodged there from when he was told of his parents death came rushing out of him. As tears streamed out of his eyes, Shanice held him close, not caring that he was wetting up her pajama top with his tears.

He wasn't aware that Shanice was crying, too, until he heard her say through her tears, "You're still my adopted brother, Trevor, and I'll never leave you. 'One for each other and each other for one,' right?"

"Right." Trevor could only agree, because it seemed as if the one thing that would never change would be the commitment they'd made to each other as orphans.

········●·········

Trevor hated that the topic of conversation after David and Elena's funeral became "who will take the orphan boy they adopted?" The Baileys, as his godparents, had been the most likely candidates, but Isaiah and Brenda had inquired and were not qualified to take him since they now had the twins, another foster child, and Shanice in a house that was considered too small to add another adoptive child.

Trevor's preference would've been the Baileys, if for no other reason than to be spared this conversation. However, David's and Elena's parents called the meeting immediately following the gathering of friends and family after the funeral where, like it or not, he was a witness to their heated debate.

"Connie and I live in a retirement home," David's father, Robert said. "Hardly the kind place for a teenager." A thin, wiry man with wispy salt and pepper hair, who couldn't seem to stand still, he paced the floor incessantly as he spoke.

"Maureen, what about you and Edgar?" Grandma Connie addressed Elena's parents. She was the opposite of her husband, a matronly woman of average height. "Can you take him?"

"We already have our daughter Nina and her three children living with us," Edgar said. "We're packed to the gills as it is." Elena's father was the most grandfatherly of the two, because he actually engaged Trevor when he was around.

"Can't you two move into David and Elena's house and take care of him?" Maureen said. Elena's mother didn't look as much like a grandmother as Grandma Connie, because she was still slender enough to look younger.

"And lose our rent-controlled condo in the city? We can't go back to taking care of lawns and homeowner's fees and the like." Robert was adamant.

"Listen, I'll take the kid," Philip said. "It makes more sense because I have no attachments, and he can move into my condo where there's plenty of room."

"What about the house?" Connie clutched conspicuously absent pearls.

"We can put the house on the market. This way he'll at least stay in Orlando, go to the same school, and what not." For someone who acted as if he could care less most of the time, Philip had a few ideas mapped out in advance, it seemed.

Edgar was the first adult to speak directly to Trevor about any of it. "So what do you think, Trevor? Would you like to go and stay with your Uncle Philip?"

The answer was an emphatic *no,* but Trevor realized he was out of options, especially if there was any hope of him staying close to Shanice and the Baileys. This solution would have to do for now.

"Yeah, I guess," Trevor said. He wasn't quite sure his selfish uncle had the ability to parent anyone. Given his choices now, he'd take what he could get over being fostered by strangers again, and possibly having to move far away from Orlando which had essentially become his home,

"Then it's settled," Philip said with a smile that Trevor didn't quite believe was genuine.

Chapter Five

When Philip stepped up, it seemed like the answer to all their prayers, especially Trevor's. The day he moved in with Philip paled in comparison to when he'd moved in with David and Elena. At least materially, it did.

Philip escorted Trevor to his room, swung the door open and waved an arm like he was a spokesmodel.

"And this is where you'll be crashing." Philip said. "Go on in and make yourself at home."

Trevor tried not to show how excited he was, but he couldn't help but return Philip's grin when he saw the state-of-the-art computer equipment in his room, together with the desktops and monitors he already owned courtesy of the Kyles.

"Go on," Philip said. "Take her for a spin, then after you unpack, we'll order some takeout."

While the computers were booting up, Trevor checked out the video game systems, both a PlayStation 3 and an XBox 360 with a video game library that would make the average kid's mouth water.

Even the furniture smelled new. After test driving his new computer equipment, he wheeled his luggage over to the closet and opened the door. Surprisingly, there were a few new clothes already hanging inside in his size.

"Wow!" Trevor said, as he riffled through the cool jeans, t-shirts, and light jackets bearing names that he knew were more expensive than the Old Navy gear the Kyles had been fond of. Maybe staying with his Uncle Phil wouldn't be all bad. Trevor missed David and Elena so much he felt guilty being sucked in by all the cool stuff he was getting now that they were gone.

He logged off the computers and put away his things. Being on the computer reminded him so much of David he didn't want to do any serious programming at the moment. After he put all his belongings away, he went in search of his uncle. The possibility of food usually made him excited enough to put away some serious grub, but not with the memories of David and Elena bombarding him even as he performed mundane tasks like folding his shirts and socks the way Elena had shown him, and hiding his browsing trail on the computer like David had shown him.

When he entered the kitchen, Phil wasn't alone as he'd expected. A buxom blonde was wound around his torso.

"Excuse me," Trevor said and ducked back out the door. He was halfway back down the hall when after hurried fumbling his uncle called out to him.

"Hey, Trev, man come back. I want you to meet somebody."

Trevor didn't want to make nice with his uncle's flavor-of-the-month, as David and Elena called Philip's friends on more than one occasion when they thought Trevor wasn't paying attention. His uncle's womanizing was one of the things he and his brother had not seen eye-to-eye on.

Trevor shuffled back toward the kitchen and re-entered. This time the woman was sitting on one of the barstools, and Phil was standing next to her, his arm draped around her shoulders.

"Trevor, this is Stacee, with a double-e. Stacee, my nephew, and now foster son, Trevor Kyle."

Trevor didn't particularly like how Philip cavalierly assumed their situation was permanent. He and, especially Shanice were still hoping the Bailey's foster child would get adopted so he could move in with them. Trevor kept his face impassive as Stacee spoke to him.

"Hi, Trevor," she said in an inordinately high-pitched voice. "Nice to meet you."

"Hello, Ms. Stacee," Trevor said, remembering how the Kyles had taught him to address his elders.

"You can drop the Ms." she said. "I'm just plain old Stacee."

"Yeah, Trevor, we don't have those kinds of rules around here. Dave and Elena were fantastic parents, but hey, I'm just barely over thirty. A little more than twice your age, but young enough you don't have to be so formal."

"Okay," Trevor said.

Phil leaned in and tongue-kissed Stacee so thoroughly, it made Trevor uncomfortable. Finally, he peeled himself away from Stacee and grabbed the phone.

"You like Chinese, Trevor?" Philip asked as he dialed.

Trevor wondered if Phil would've changed if he'd said no, but he didn't bother. Chinese was great when he had an appetite. He wasn't sure whether he'd be hungry once the food arrived, so he answered in the affirmative.

Stacee jutted her ample chest out and smiled at Trevor. She had a childlike quality about her, despite her very mature-looking body and state of dress. Trevor's hormones responded in the manner in which they were designed. Thankfully he was wearing baggy shorts over tightey-whiteys or he might've had an embarrassing situation to explain. Even so, Trevor turned away and headed back to his room when Phil got off the phone and glued himself to Stacee again. He would get dinner later. Or not.

··········●···········

In the beginning, Philip appeared to be just as nice and caring as his brother. Well, at least his generosity trumped everything David and Elena had done for Trevor, and early on that was the only barometer by which he was able to measure the difference. It was easy for a kid coming from poverty such as his to have his head turned by expensive things. Plus Uncle Philip was cool, and Trevor was in hog heaven for all of two weeks before the other shoe dropped.

"Hey little buddy," Uncle Philip said one evening after he'd gotten home from school. "Here's your allowance for the month."

Philip handed him a crisp one hundred dollar bill. "There's more where that came from. I might just need you to pitch in and help your old uncle out with some work I'll be bringing home every once in a while."

"What kind of work?" Trevor held the money by one corner as if it might burn him.

"Some special computer work that only an expert like you can help me with."

Trevor mentally puffed his chest out at being called an expert at first, but then his brow furrowed. "Don't they have IT people at the bank where you work?"

"They do, but they're doing other things with their time. The bank expects me to know this computer crap, but the fact is I don't."

"I could teach you a few things, I guess," Trevor said, finally pocketing the bill.

"I think it would be better if you did them," Philip said. "Don't you want to pull a little weight around here? I know David and Elena taught you that it's a good thing to help out. To pay your keep, so to speak."

"Yeah, they did." Trevor said. That sounded logical, so Trevor would go with it. What harm would it be to help his computer illiterate uncle out?

"All I need is for you to find some information on people for me every once in a while on the internet," Phil said. "These are people I'm investigating for my work."

"What kind of information do you need?"

"Full names, addresses, banking information, social security numbers."

"David said it's unethical to have access to people's personal information like that."

"Not if you work where I work," Philip said. Philip was a CPA who worked in one of the banks that held the state of Florida's unclaimed property funds. "And you're helping me do my work, so there won't be any need to share this with anyone else, right?"

"I guess."

"I'll tell you what. You do this work for me from time to time, you get double the allowance I just gave you. Also, you can stay up as long as you want at night, just so you get up and go to school. Deal?"

What teenaged boy wouldn't enjoy rules relaxed to non-existence, no formal bedtime, and an allowance big enough to bankroll whatever vices he could buy before coming of age to sample them as a matter of course?

Trevor's reluctance was overruled by his desire to stay up and watch some late night skin flicks on his Uncle's cable. "Deal."

"I'll bring the first list tomorrow," Philip said. "They have money sitting in the state coffers that I want to get back to them, so you'll be doing these folks a favor."

Easy peasy. Trevor didn't feel like he had the right to question any further at the time, since Philip did work at a bank. Besides he was an adult, a banking professional, and must know better about the legality of such things.

"Okay. I'm gonna go do my homework," Trevor said, his mind now on the first of many adult films he would get to watch while under Philip's care.

Trevor took the huge allowances, the money making it easy for him to get into other things no middle school child should have access to. The most taboo of them was watching dirty movies, until he began to hang out at Phil's adult parties.

Chapter Six

"Hey, Trevor, are we still going to see the new Spiderman movie this weekend?"

Trevor hit his forehead with the heel of his free hand, almost dropping his cell phone. "Aw, 'Nice, I've got to help my Uncle Philip with some stuff this weekend."

"But you promised."

Her disappointment pierced his heart, but he didn't want to miss what was shaping up to be an epic party.

If his uncle wasn't frequenting the local casinos he loved so much, or out of town under the guise of working to check out the bigger casinos in Las Vegas and Atlantic City, the condo became party central. This Saturday night Phil had hired not one, but three strippers.

Philip didn't think there was anything wrong with having his teenaged charge hanging around with the party girls and strippers he and his friends entertained. Trevor became exposed to things he would never have seen at his age if David and Elena were still alive. Hormonal teenager that he was, Trevor didn't see anything wrong with it at the moment, either.

"I'll tell you what, Shanice. Let's go to Epcot Center tomorrow afternoon." He knew that park was her favorite, and it would be the only way to make up for missing the movie premiere. That would also give him some time to get over any residual hangover he might have from the party tonight.

"Okay, but you can't complain no matter how long I spend in each of the countries."

"I promise not to complain." He'd gladly spend as much time as she wanted as long as he didn't get to miss seeing three real live women shuck their clothes tonight.

"You think Brenda or Isaiah could give us a ride?" Trevor knew Philip would be so hung over, he would just barely make it to work on time Monday, let alone drive a couple of kids to a theme park.

"I'll get Dad to do it, Mom's been puking her guts out all morning. She thinks she's got stomach flu."

"Really? Then you'd better stay away from her," Trevor said. "That stuff is catching."

"No way am I going to miss going to Epcot tomorrow. I'll let Dad take care of her today. I'll just do some cleaning around the house to help out."

"Okay, see you tomorrow, squirt."

"Bye."

Philip came into the back door carrying a case of beer just as Trevor hung up with Shanice.

"Hey buddy, can you help me get the rest of the stuff out of the car?"

"Sure thing." Trevor pocketed his cell phone and helped bring in several gallons of liquor, several more cases of beer and a couple of kegs. It seemed like a lot, but he knew that sometime before midnight someone would have to make another run for booze. Phil's parties always required more booze.

Trevor often pilfered beer and consumed it in his room away from any adults who might take exception to him partaking at his age. Philip couldn't care less, but there was usually some do-gooder female who tried to shame Philip into making Trevor stop drinking, so he didn't drink in front of the party-goers anymore.

Shortly after they got all the booze and party food in, Stacee showed up, but this time she wasn't alone. There was a girl with her who looked like a younger version of herself without the enhanced boobs and tons of makeup.

Stacee jumped Philip's bones practically the moment she entered the room and didn't see fit to make any introductions. Trevor and the new girl, who didn't look to be much older than him, eyed each other for a while, before she finally got the courage to introduce herself.

"Hi, I'm Tracee, Stacee's sister."

"I'm Trevor, Philip's nephew."

She eyed her sister and Phil going at it. "Are they always like this?"

Trevor snorted. "Yeah, pretty much."

Tracee made a gagging motion. "I would tell them to get a room, but it's his house."

"Yeah, right." Trevor shoved his hands into his pockets. "You wanna play some video games in my room? Phil's guests won't be arriving for another hour or so."

"Sure, why not," Tracee said. "Lead the way."

Trevor loved the reaction he got to his room from the few visitors he'd had since he moved in with Philip. None matched Tracee's.

"Wow! This is quite the set-up you've got here, Trevor."

"Thanks." His reaction was sheepish, in spite of himself.

Tracee touched the equipment as she looked around. "What do you do?"

"I'm a programmer." He remembered David's advice to never tell anyone he was a hacker. And clearly Tracee assumed he was older, otherwise she would've asked him something like what school he went to.

At fourteen, he was already almost six feet tall and wasn't finished growing yet. He would play it cool with Tracee and see what happened. The night was young.

"Okay, so program something for me."

Trevor grinned. "Okay."

He booted up his system and settled into his desk chair. Tracee hovered over his shoulder, but she didn't bother him when she did it as much as it bothered him when Philip did.

He created a simple wallpaper with her name on it, but he spelled it Tracey.

"Oh, it's Tracee with two E's. Our mother thought it was cute to give me and Stacee similar sounding names." She frowned.

Trevor changed the spelling of her name and showed her the result. "If you'll give me your email address, I'll send it to you."

"Okay."

While he was opening his email to send the wallpaper to her, Tracee headed back toward the door. "I'm going to get something to drink. What's your poison?"

"Poison?"

Trevor was confused, but Tracee took it to mean he was distracted. "What do you want to drink?"

"A beer." Trevor realized he'd have to pay attention or he'd make an ass out of himself and ruin the charade. If Tracee was anything like her sister, he figured if he played his cards right, he could get lucky.

Chapter Seven

"Want another?" Tracee stood, grabbing their empties.

Trevor was pulverizing her on the video games, so he didn't blame her for getting bored. He decided he'd cool it and let her win when she returned. "Yeah, sure."

Even with his beer buzz he was a formidable opponent on any video game, so he couldn't blame Tracee for sucking at it.

When she returned with a six-pack this time, she also had a backpack slung over one shoulder.

"Hey, do you mind if I change in your bathroom in a little while?" She scrunched up her face when she said it, looking so cute, Trevor would've said yes to anything at that moment.

"Uh, No. Not at all." It excited him that it looked like she planned to spend the night, too. Stacee stayed over quite a bit, so it wasn't illogical.

Tracee dropped her book bag on Trevor's bed and set four of the beers on the dresser, giving Trevor one and keeping one for herself. "So, is it my turn?" She squinted at the television.

"Yeah," he said. "The aliens killed me."

She took her gamechair and picked up the controller with both hands. While she was gone, Trevor had changed the mode on the game to beginner because if the skill level had remained where they began, she would never win.

As Tracee picked off aliens with her various weapons, she grew more and more excited. By the time she killed the last one on that level, she was bouncing in her seat. Her smallish breasts jiggled with every movement. Trevor was mesmerized.

When she won, she jumped up and threw her arms into the air like she'd just won a prize fight. Her halter scooted up, showing even more of her abdomen, and revealing a pierced navel. Trevor had seen girls like her on his late night television, but having one in his room was another thing altogether.

He'd been operating with a semi boner ever since she'd arrived, but the last few seconds had him painfully stretched out in his jeans. This did not go unnoticed by Tracee. Her mouth twisted into a sexy smirk, which in the movies Trevor watched, usually meant the guy was about to score. He hoped against hope that would be the case for him.

On one of Tracee's many forays back to the kitchen for beer, Trevor had borrowed a couple of condoms from Philip's stash. He had learned in health class that these were necessary to prevent disease and pregnancy. Two things he really didn't need at his age. His mother's struggles with him and his sister had taught him that.

Trevor watched as Tracee sashayed to the door and locked it. She sauntered back over to him, her hips swaying in a more exaggerated motion than they had all night. On the way over to him, she loosened the top of her halter and it fell, releasing a set of real, live breasts. All creamy white with pink nipples. Trevor almost came in his pants.

He scrubbed a hand over his face and into his hair. *Calm down, Kyle. Be cool.*

Tracee straddled him on his game chair and his hands glommed onto her breasts like magnets. Then he remembered how the guys fondled them in the movies he'd seen and he mimicked their actions. Tracee kissed him hard, thrusting her tongue into his mouth and arresting his. He followed her lead and wrestled her tongue with his own, while simultaneously teasing her nipples with his thumbs, cupping them with his hands. He manipulated them like the toggle switch on a game controller, but it felt so much better. His dick attested to the excruciating sensations by growing infinitely harder, and then all bets were off, he needed to be inside her like yesterday.

Trevor stood and Tracee held on as he moved them quickly to his bed where they fell in a heap, mouths locked and hands ripping clothes from their bodies, stopping only when his t-shirt needed to be pulled over his head and when they both removed pants. Trevor forgot about protection, he was so painfully hard, but Tracee didn't. She rummaged into his bedside table and found the condoms he'd stashed there and had one rolled onto him practically before he could blink, then pulled him down into her hot wetness.

The sensation made his eyes roll involuntarily, it felt so good to be sheathed by what he'd only fantasized about up until that point. Tracee knew what she was doing as she rolled her banging body against his, taking him deeper and deeper until he felt he was winding up to be consumed by her. Trevor didn't care. He'd stay there and be consumed if he could keep feeling what he was feeling, but his body had other ideas. His orgasm rendered him almost boneless as he exploded into the condom, the warmth of his own jizz and the clenching of her muscles milking him until he was spent.

Only two weeks away from his fifteenth birthday, Trevor had no idea that Tracee had not experienced the same feelings he had until she took his hand and showed him how to help her to an orgasm since he'd finished so fast. He hadn't been able to help it, and he kind of felt bad that she didn't get to scream and writhe while he was inside her like the women in movies he saw. However, after a few minutes of touching her down there, she tensed up and squelched her scream, even though the music was so loud no one would've heard her anyway.

Trevor watched her facial expression and her body's reaction as she came and she looked just like the women he'd seen in the movies. Then she opened her eyes and grinned up at him.

"That was your first time, wasn't it?" She asked.

He thought to lie, but then he figured if he were honest, she might take pity on him and want to do it again. "Yeah. How'd you know?"

"You had a one-track mind like most guys your age. The goal being: To. Get. In. There!" She grinned, punctuating each word. "But what you lacked in technique, you made up for in sheer size and enthusiasm."

Trevor fleetingly wondered how old she thought he was, but he wasn't about to ask. He couldn't help the grin that sprouted on his face or the pride he felt in her approval of his assets.

Just as he moved in to kiss her, there was a loud knocking on his door. "What the fuck?" Trevor spat in irritation.

Tracee giggled, then looked at the clock on his bedside table. "Oh shit! I'm supposed to dance tonight."

"Dance?" Trevor said. "You want me to dance with you?" Shanice had taught him some moves, so he felt he could keep up with Tracee on the dance floor.

Tracee flat out laughed at that one. "Not that kind of dancing silly. I'm part of tonight's entertainment."

To say he was surprised was an understatement. He knew that Stacee danced at a club downtown, but Tracee did not look like Stacee and most of her friends. She looked young and wholesome.

Trevor scratched a sudden itch behind his ear. "You... ?" He didn't get to finish his question, because the pounding began again, this time accompanied by Philip's irritated voice.

"Trevor! Open the damn door!"

Trevor rolled off the bed and pulled on his jeans. Tracee rolled off on the other side, grabbed her backpack and disappeared into the bathroom. Philip pushed into the door as soon as he heard Trevor turn the lock, and stumbled into the room. Trevor closed the door behind him.

Philip took in the rumpled bed, the video game on pause and the beer bottles. Then he sniffed. "Smells like somebody's been fucking in here." He got a stern look on his face.

Trevor began to babble. "It was ... me and Tracee were fooling around and ... it just... "

"Calm the fuck down, little buddy." Grinning, Philip socked him in the shoulder. Hard. "You just got your first piece. Good going."

"Really?"

"Yeah. I've been meaning to talk to you about that, but looks like you've got the mechanics down. Just remember to wrap it up, yeah?"

"Wrap it up?"

"Wear a condom?" Philip looked into his eyes to make sure he understood what he was saying.

"Oh, yeah, they told us that at school, and I borrowed some of yours."

Philip cackled. "But I don't want 'em back."

Trevor laughed because Philip's laughter while he was drunk was kind of infectious.

"She get off, too? Because chicks are more generous when you get them off."

"Yeah, she did."

Trevor hung his head sheepishly, but then raised his chin and folded his arms as Tracee came out of the bathroom wearing what had to be her dancing outfit. She was dressed like a Catholic schoolgirl except with a shorter skirt, complete with ponytails. Trevor's dick got hard again, and he hoped Tracee was up to going again once her number was over.

······●······

There was always gambling at Philip's parties, which drew quite the unsavory crowd. Trevor had been around enough such characters when he'd been with his mother to recognize them, and knew to steer clear.

Most of the guys, however, were like Phil. Youngish working stiffs looking for a little action. Trevor masqueraded as one of them, and Philip, surprisingly didn't blow his cover. Especially since he seemed so proud that Trevor had lost his virginity.

Trevor watched Tracee perform, wondering how these men managed not to embarrass themselves when they were around all these sexy party girls all the time.

Tracee worked the room, teasing the men and enraging some of the women until she was down to just pasties and a thong. Then as her finale she danced over to Trevor and kissed him square on the lips and ran off back into his room. A couple of the guys ribbed him about her and Trevor took it good-naturedly, then went back into his room in search of her.

He heard the shower running as he entered the room and closed the door. The bathroom door was cracked open as if in invitation. He slumped into a game chair and turned on the console.

"Trevor?" Tracee called from the bathroom.

Trevor turned the game console off and jumped up, moving closer to the door to hear better. "Yeah?"

"Can you wash my back?"

That was all the invitation he needed. He entered the bathroom shucking his clothes.

Chapter Eight

Trevor waited out in front of the condo for Isaiah and Shanice to pick him up Sunday afternoon. Thankfully, he'd gone relatively light on the drinking and gotten high on a little weed and the sexual prowess of Tracee Douglas. So he was more than happy to spend an afternoon in the company of his surrogate sister. Hopefully this would make up for the other times he'd stood her up.

Isaiah pulled up to the curb, and Shanice climbed over the console to let him have the front seat. He settled in and they took off.

Shanice had dressed up in her best and brightest short set, and even had on a bit of clear lip gloss.

"You look nice, squirt," Trevor said.

She rolled her eyes, but smiled all the same. "Thanks."

"You hoping to see Owen Nettles at the park today?" Owen was a boy she'd told Trevor and her parents about a few months before, who'd given her an elaborate Valentine's gift and since then had been making goo-goo eyes at her.

"Oh, shut up, Trevor. You know I don't like him like that."

Trevor and Isaiah both laughed.

"How's it going, Trev?" Isaiah said, careful to keep his eyes on the road as they wove into traffic on a busy thoroughfare.

"Great!" Trevor hoped he didn't sound too enthusiastic. The last couple of times he'd spoken to Isaiah and Brenda about Philip, he had not been singing the guy's praises.

Isaiah turned to look at him in the eye. "Is this the same young man who's been unhappy at Casa de Philippe all summer?"

"Aw, Uncle Phil's not so bad," Trevor said. "I guess I just had to get to know him. You know what I mean?"

"I know what you mean." Isaiah's eyes squinted as they locked on Trevor's neck.

"What?" Trevor said.

"Nothing." Isaiah shook his head. "We have some great news, though. Brenda and I are expecting another child."

"Really? That is great," Trevor said. "So, you ready for another little brother or sister, Shanice?"

"Yes, it's going to be a little girl, so I won't be the only one."

"We'll be thankful for either," Isaiah said. "Although Shanice is convinced it's a girl."

"I dreamed I had a little sister. The stork brought her."

"Um, you know that's not how it works, right?" Isaiah said.

"Yeah," Shanice said. "But I'm not sure about the real way it happens."

"Your mom and I will talk to you about it later, okay? But first, I think I might need to have a conversation with Trevor about it."

Trevor was appalled. "Why me?"

"There's evidence that you might be engaged in some activities, that could produce just such a situation."

"What situation?" Shanice said. "Are you talking about sex?"

"Not to you at the moment," Isaiah said. "Hold up, I'm going to stop at McDonald's right up here to use the bathroom. I guess I drank too much coffee at the service this morning."

"TMI, Dad," Shanice said.

Trevor grinned nervously. Then he remembered where Isaiah's eyes were trained and lowered the visor to look at himself in the mirror.

Fuck! He had a hickey. Tracee had been so enthusiastic during their shower and afterward, she had sucked on his fair skin too hard.

Isaiah parked the car. "Anybody else need to take a bathroom break?"

Both Trevor and Shanice shook their heads.

"You want a drink or something, 'Nice?"

"Yes. Thanks, Dad."

Isaiah then turned to Trevor. "Want to come with, Trevor?"

"Nah, I'm good." Trevor's mouth was suddenly dry, but he wasn't about to let Isaiah know.

"Come on," Isaiah coaxed. "You can bring Shanice's drink back."

"Okay." Trevor got out and followed Isaiah into the McDonald's and they got into the line behind the last person.

"So, what did you do this weekend?" Isaiah asked. "Did you go out with friends, yesterday? Because Shanice thought you and she were going to see Spiderman."

Trevor shook his head. "I didn't go out, and I'm sorry I had to disappoint Shanice, but Uncle Phil had a party, so I stuck around to help him out."

"And did one of his friends help you out?"

"What do you mean?"

"How'd you get the hickey, son?"

Trevor's face grew warm, and he was sure he was some very alarming shade of red. "From this girl. Uh, Phil's girlfriend, Stacee's little sister." Trevor hoped his description of her as Stacee's little sister would get Isaiah off his back. However, Tracee was nineteen and would be twenty soon. He knew intuitively that this was not information that would go over well with Isaiah, so he withheld it.

"Listen, Trevor. You're a young man and I know your hormones have kicked in big time, and David probably didn't get a chance to have a talk with you about things, but I'll be happy to step in if Phil hasn't done so."

"Oh, Phil and I did have a talk, just last night." Trevor just didn't share with the good pastor the extent of that talk. "So, I'm good."

"Are you sure?" Isaiah said, skepticism written all over his face. "Because I'm trusting you with my daughter... "

Trevor's indignation bordered on anger. "I would never ... "

Isaiah cut him off with hands raised, palms out. "I know, I know. Shanice is like a little sister to you and I know I can trust you with her, but you might inadvertently expose her to things she's not ready for."

Trevor shoved his hands in his pocket and toed the floor. "I won't. I promise."

"Okay, Trevor. But next time you're making out tell the girl to go easy on your delicate skin."

Trevor didn't know whether to laugh or stay serious, but then Isaiah pointed at his own neck. "See this? Black never cracks."

And Trevor lost it, not sure if his laughter was borne of relief that he'd dodged the Pastor Isaiah Bailey bullet, or if the joke was really all that funny.

Chapter Nine

Shanice noticed the change in Trevor first, because she still saw him at school the first year he was in Philip's custody. Courtesy of Tracee Douglas' sexual tutelage, he got a bit of reputation with the girls at his high school, especially those willing to put out. Most were saving themselves, since it was a Christian school, but he didn't have to look far or long to find a girl who was willing to walk a little bit on the wild side with him.

He also had money to burn, so he got an immediate in with the "bad boys" at school. Shanice found him hanging out with boys at school who were into the stuff he'd discovered through Phil's influence, and needless to say, she didn't like it one bit.

At eleven, she was still the same Shanice she always had been: never afraid to speak her mind. She marched over to them where they were smoking a joint under a copse of trees on the edge of campus and called him out.

"Trevor!" She stood there with hands on non-existent hips.

"What do you want, Shanice?"

"What's that in your hand?"

His friends snickered. "Trevor's getting pwned by his little sister."

"She looks like a darker version of that little girl on Drake and Josh with that expression on her face," another said. They all laughed outright this time and passed the joint around.

Trevor was mortified and scared that these guys he was hanging out with were going to rag him forever for this, so he was uncharacteristically harsh. "Mind your own business, kid. Now get the fuck out of here."

She put her hand on her mouth in shock, because she'd never heard Trevor talk like that to her before. The look of hurt and betrayal on her face made Trevor feel like a first-rate asshole, but he couldn't take it back in front of his friends. Then she turned and ran away.

Trevor went by the Baileys' after school. By that time, his fleeting high was gone, and he worried Shanice would rat him out to her parents.

Brenda answered the door with one of the twins on her hip. Ezekiel and Ezra were almost two. "Hey, Trevor! Would you hold Zeke a second until I corral his brother?" She didn't seem upset or like she didn't want him to be around, so he figured Shanice hadn't said anything.

"Sure," he said and took the toddler, who squealed. "Twevor!"

"Hey, buddy," Trevor said. He closed the door and carried Zeke into the house behind Brenda, who walked briskly into the family room and scooped up Ezra, who was making circles around the furniture, and deposited him in his high chair.

Trevor sat Zeke in the high chair next to his twin. "Um, where's Shanice?"

"Homework," Brenda said as she set places at the table. "But she'll be down in a few minutes for dinner."

"Whatever it is you're cooking smells really good," he said.

"Pot roast," she said with a smile. "If you'll wash your hands and help me finish setting the table, you can join us. I worry Philip doesn't feed you well."

"He doesn't cook, but I get by. I nuke most of the stuff I want to eat." Trevor went to the sink and quickly washed his hands.

Brenda shook her head. "I keep letting you know you have an open invitation for dinner. And you don't have to stay in that house alone while Philip's out of town."

Trevor followed Brenda's example and set the rest of the places at the table. By the time he was done, Pastor Isaiah came ambling into the house, booming, "What smells so good?" He walked into the kitchen and saw Trevor. "You don't look anything like my lovely wife." Then he gave Trevor one of those guy shakes where they lean in and bump shoulders.

Trevor grinned. "She's in the kitchen, and the answer to your other question, is pot roast." Isaiah went over to greet his twins by kissing them each on the top of their heads.

"Daddy!" they squealed.

"You're staying for dinner, right?" Isaiah said as he left Trevor in the dining room with the twins.

"Yes," Trevor said. When he turned back to the twins, he saw Ezra was trying to climb out of his highchair. "Oh no you don't," Trevor said and re-seated him and adjusted the tray in front of him.

Shanice came down, yelling "Mom!" When she saw Trevor, she pursed her lips and refused to speak to him. She sauntered over to her little brothers and handed Zeke his fallen sippy cup then ruffled Ezra's hair.

She took the place setting Trevor made next to his own and moved it to the other side of the table by the twins.

"I know you're mad at me, Shanice, and you're right to be mad, but please don't tell your parents what you saw," he said quickly, before Brenda and Isaiah came in carrying dishes of food to the table.

Shanice just glared at him and took her seat then played with the twins as if Trevor weren't there.

After Isaiah said the blessing, they all dug into the meal. There was conversation around the table, but Shanice refused to address Trevor directly; She gave one-syllable answers directed at someone else, or none at all.

Brenda and Isaiah had to notice what was going on, but they didn't pry. Trevor didn't have time to be upset. This was his first home-cooked meal in a long time. Since Brenda offered, he'd make this a habit.

At the end of the meal, Trevor said, "I'll help Shanice do the dishes, Ms. Brenda."

"Oh, thanks, guys," Brenda said with a smile. "That means I can bathe the twins early and get them to bed."

"What about me?" Pastor Isaiah said and waggled his eyebrows.

"You can get your own bath," Brenda said.

"Ew!" Shanice said. "You guys are gross."

Trevor felt his face heat up.

"Someday you young people will know what it's like to have that special someone in your lives," Isaiah said and helped clear the table.

Shanice held back. "I'll carry one of the chunkies upstairs for you, Mom," she said and grabbed Zeke. Brenda took Ezra and they disappeared upstairs.

"My daughter appears to be upset with you." Isaiah said.

Trevor should have seen this coming. "Yes, sir."

"What did you do? Honestly, anything you did was wrong from the word go, but you want to talk about it?"

"Well, I was with some guys at school today and Shanice interrupted us." He left out the part about what they were doing. "I may have hurt her feelings when I asked her to leave us alone."

"I know you're growing up, Trevor, and Shanice still has a ways to go, but she has always idolized you, since our Baptist Home days. Go easy on my baby girl, or I might have to slap your face with a glove and challenge you to a duel."

Trevor grinned. "I can't duel without a weapon."

"Who said anything about weapons?" Isaiah put up his fists. "I'm talking about duking it out the old fashioned way." He jabbed in the air in Trevor's direction a couple times, and Trevor played along, dodging his fists.

"I was going to apologize while we were doing the dishes, but she went upstairs."

"She'll come back down in a little while. You know she can't stay mad at you."

Trevor hoped Isaiah was right, because it was just miserable having Shanice mad at him. They'd just finished loading the dishwasher when Shanice came back down, and Isaiah retired to the den. He said it was to watch CNN, but Trevor knew he was giving them some privacy.

"'Nice," Trevor said. "I'm sorry."

Shanice didn't respond. Not even to his nickname for her. She took her book and sat down at the dining room table then flipped it open.

Trevor took a seat in the chair beside her and tried again. "'Nice?"

Isaiah yelled, "Shanice, put that boy out of his misery and accept his apology. You'll learn later in life that as a gender collectively, we tend to sometimes say stupid things." Trevor heard the TV turn off, then Isaiah headed upstairs, but not before he yelled, "I'll drive you home when you're ready, Trevor."

Trevor felt really stupid now, but he'd do anything to not have Shanice mad at him. "What you saw me doing earlier... I quit. I promise. And I won't use bad words around you anymore. I don't want Pastor Isaiah and Ms. Brenda to stop me from coming around."

Shanice put her book down and looked up at him. "You hurt my feelings, Trevor," she said, and her bottom lip trembled. "Don't do it again."

"I won't," he promised, not altogether sure he would be able to keep that promise.

Chapter Ten

It wasn't until six months later, when Philip lost his job that he began to ask Trevor to do things that made him increasingly uncomfortable. Phillip took trips to Atlantic City and Las Vegas, whereas before he traveled the shorter distances to Hollywood, Florida and Biloxi, Mississippi. VIP cards from the casinos began to come in the mail. Then, rather than make up stories, Phillip just flat out told Trevor to take his clients' money.

"I need you to move the funds from the people on this list and make it where no one knows it's you, just like David said you could," Philip said.

"Why? You know that's not legal, Uncle Philip."

"Are you questioning my authority? I'm your guardian. I pay all the fucking bills around here, keep your greedy mouth fed, and buy you all this top-of-the-line computer shit. How dare you question me?"

Trevor did it a few times more before he hacked into Philip's personal accounts to see why he needed so much cash. A large chunk of the insurance money that David and Elena had left to take care of Trevor was gone, except his college fund. Philip couldn't touch that, thank goodness. Trevor was looking forward to college as his opportunity to escape.

Until then, unless he was working on something for Philip, he camped out at the Baileys' house most of the time. Isaiah questioned him about Philip one evening after dinner. They were barbequing on the patio out back that overlooked the pool.

"How are things with you and Philip?" Isaiah asked. "He's gone an awful lot. I mean, we love having you here, but I just want to make sure you're being properly cared for."

"Uncle Philip gambles," Trevor said, no longer willing to keep Philip's dirty little secret. "A lot."

"Oh?" Isaiah said. "I wonder how DCFS missed that little detail about him. I'll make some inquiries."

"If they take me away from Philip, they could send me anywhere in the state. Please don't do anything that will get me taken far away, so I won't get to see you guys," Trevor said. "Uncle Philip isn't the worst foster parent I've ever had, and when I go away to college, I'll never have to see him again if I don't want to." He didn't want to tell Isaiah about the other illegal stuff he was doing, because he'd definitely call DCFS about that, and he didn't know how much trouble he'd be in.

"That may be true, but Brenda and I worry about you with him. David told me about Philip's behavior when they were growing up, but I thought he'd matured enough to give you a stable home. Never hesitate to tell us if it gets too bad, okay?"

"Okay," Trevor said.

Isaiah called DCFS anyway and a caseworker came out snooping around. It just so happened that Uncle Phil was on his best behavior that week. It was almost as if he'd been tipped off they were coming, because he hired a cleaning company to come out and give the condo a thorough once-over and even cooked dinner every day. When questioned about his gambling, Phil pretended to break down.

"I had a problem," he admitted. "But I'm going to get help." He showed the case worker some information from his employee assistance program from his job. The caseworker though skeptical, left with a promise to return often until she was satisfied Phil was back on the straight and narrow.

A few months later, Philip had worked through the rest of the insurance money. He decided then that people who allowed funds to go unclaimed didn't care about their finances, and these people should be targeted, since they were so careless with their money.

As gambling became Philip's pastime and primary means of support, he kept going to loan sharks. The loan sharks were used to bankroll his gambling habit, and the thefts from unclaimed property accounts kept things going when he couldn't pay the loan sharks. Trevor felt more and more trapped, but he knew if he went to the authorities, he could be taken out of Philip's custody, and put back into the system.

Hired muscle for the loan sharks came around and roughed up Philip when he couldn't pay. Trevor always dreaded this, since right after a beat-down, Philip would make him do more funneling from the unclaimed accounts.

"Hey Trev?"

Trevor had grown to hate the pet name Elena had given him simply because Philip used it. "What?" Trevor was unable to answer with any respect. The man didn't deserve it.

"Watch your tone, son."

"I'm not your son," Trevor said, unable to stop himself.

"Thank God," Philip said. "As long as you do as I say, I'll keep a roof over your head and clothes and on your no-good back, but you'll do what I tell you to do." Philip handed him a list. "Hack into these accounts and take several thousand out of each. Clean up like you always do, because I don't want the feds snooping around."

OBSIDIAN FAITH • 56

Trevor must have taken too long to take the list from his hand, because Philip pulled him out of his chair and held him up by the scruff of his collar. "When I tell you to do something, you will answer me in a respectful tone. Do you hear me?"

Trevor wanted to push it, but all it would do was cause his uncle to punish him physically. At sixteen now, Trevor had stopped caring about his uncle and his tirades.

"I'm going to tell Pastor Bailey and Ms. Brenda about this, so they can get custody of me. I'm tired of stealing for you."

Philip tightened his hold on Trevor's collar, and his nostrils flared. "If you breathe a word to the Baileys, or anyone, about this, you'll be sorry. As sorry as my dead brother and his wife."

That scared him. His uncle was intimating that he'd had something to do with David and Elena's death. It sickened Trevor to hear that.

"You know, it would be easy for me to hurt that little play sister of yours, too—." Philip said. "She could disappear one day, and the Baileys would never see her again. You either, boy. So get your attitude together."

Trevor was really afraid of what his uncle might do. If Philip hurt Shanice, it would be all his fault, and he couldn't live with that. For the first time, he hated how stupid he'd been to help Philip out the first time. He should've refused, because now he was trapped. Trevor was sure those guys his uncle was hanging with all were part of some organized crime outfit. He'd watched enough of the Sopranos to know about the mob. His uncle had told them about his computer abilities, and they brought him small jobs to do.

The two tough guys who were around the most, the ones he'd nicknamed Frick and Frack, were sort of like the cartoon characters, *Pinky and The Brain*. One was tall, lanky, and feeble-minded, and the other was a short, stocky, vicious schemer.

"Hey kid," the short one, Frick, said to him one day. "Our boss wants you to work on the program that runs his slot machines. He needs you to make it more difficult for anyone to win but leave a few loose, so we can keep the suckers coming. Can you do that?"

"Why would I want to do that?" Trevor said. "I get caught, I'm going to Juvie."

The little man glared at him. "Phil told us how you cover your tracks when you take for him, so you do the same thing for us, or else you might get into that nice little car Philip's giving you, and the brakes will go out, or a bomb might go off."

Trevor didn't care. He'd almost prefer it, he was so sick of all of it. "You do what you want to me. I don't give a damn."

Frick and Frack worked Trevor over that day until he passed out. They'd been careful not to injure his face so he could go to school, or his hands so he could type, but his gut felt like someone had put him through a meat tenderizer, and he was sure one of his ribs might have been cracked. Even that didn't shake his resolve, but what did was coming to with pictures of the Baileys with bull's-eyes drawn on them taped to the walls of his bedroom.

Chapter Eleven

Trevor decided then he would distance himself from the Baileys. He stopped visiting their home and didn't stay with them when his uncle was out of town. The next time his uncle threatened Shanice, Trevor told him he didn't care about her or anybody. He hoped it would be enough to keep Phil's focus off the Baileys, especially if he could convince his uncle they weren't important to him anymore.

That hope was short-lived. Soon Phil owed the mob so much money, the state of Florida alone wasn't enough. His uncle checked him out of school one day to share an ingenious plan he and Frick and Frack had cooked up.

As Trevor approached Phil's car that day, he saw the mobsters waiting in the car, one in the front passenger side and one in the backseat. Phil opened his door, but Trevor just stood there, wondering if he shouldn't run.

Where would he go, though? The Baileys were out of the question if he didn't want to put their lives in jeopardy.

"What're you waiting for?" Frack said. "Get in the goddamn car."

"Trevor," Philip said in warning.

Trevor had no choice. He got in and Philip pulled away.

"So, here's the deal," Frick said. "Back when Phil told us where he gets his money from, that got us thinking. If we expand this little operation to a couple other states, we could give Florida a rest while we fleece some new ones."

"You can do that can't you, kid?" Frack said.

"'Course he can," Phil said. "My nephew is a computer genius."

Trevor was not in a mood to be patronized that day, so he decided he'd stall them. "I don't have the inside access that I had when I started doing this for Phil. Going in blind trying to do this in another state is going to take a while."

"How long?" Frick said.

"It could take months to hack into the list alone. Then I'd have to find out which banks they used, and that could take several more months."

Frack pointed a finger in his face. "Listen, you're not jerking us around, are you, kid?"

"No. I promise," Trevor lied.

"In the meantime, the Boss has got some more slot machines he wants you to fix for him."

Trevor got a sick feeling in the pit of his stomach. He did the slot job, and he "started" on the other job, when in fact he was just farting around on the internet feigning the work for the other states. David once told him that when hackers did things across state lines, that was automatic federal time. He would try to stay within the confines of federal law a little while longer.

· · · · · · · · · ●· · · · · · · · · · ·

"T-t-trevor... "

Shanice was crying so hard on the phone he could barely understand anything except his name. His resolve to stay away from the Baileys went out the window when he heard that little girl crying.

"Hey, Shanice. What's wrong?"

There was more sobbing before she said, "It's Mom... ."

Trevor's mind immediately went to Frick and Frack. What If they'd done something to Brenda to send him a message? "Okay, you need to calm down and breathe so I can understand what you're saying. What happened to Brenda?"

"S-she was in an a-accident."

"Where are you?"

"At home with the twins. Dad's at the hospital with Mom. S-she lost the baby, Trevor. It was a little girl."

"I'm on my way."

Trevor didn't care that he just had a learner's permit. He took the car Phil promised him for his birthday that he wasn't supposed to be driving alone yet, and drove the few miles to the Bailey's home. Their neighbor's dog began to bark like Trevor was a stranger, despite the fact he'd been a resident of that street when they got him.

He called Shanice rather than use the doorbell to let her know he was there. The twins were probably in bed, so he didn't want to wake them. A few seconds later, she opened the door and ran straight into his arms.

"Trevor. I'm so glad you came. I'm so sad." She was so overwrought she was trembling. "And I've missed you so much."

"I know, squirt. Let's go inside so the neighbor's dog'll stop yapping."

When they got inside and sat on the sofa together, Trevor tried to get some further answers to the questions he had.

"Do you know what happened?"

"We'd come home from lunch after church and Mom fed the boys and bathed them, but she said she needed something to add to the casserole she was making for dinner, so she went to the grocery store."

Shanice's eyes got glassy as she was telling him the story. "She just went to the Publix around the corner to grab a few things. After she'd been gone an hour, Dad got worried and took his truck to go look for her.

"He called me back ten minutes later and told me he was on his way to the hospital. Mom's van was being towed when he got there, so he asked some of the folks standing around what had happened. They said a beat-up, black jeep with two men in it ran a red-light and hit her van on the driver's side."

That was confirmation it was Frick and Frack. Frick owned an old black jeep that he called his fishing truck. He usually didn't drive it when he was around Phil's, but Trevor had seen it once when they went to work on their boss's slots.

"Dad called me an hour later from the hospital and told me Mom had lost the baby."

"Is Brenda okay, though?" Trevor asked anxiously.

"Dad said she had a broken leg, and they were going to do something to stop her from bleeding from the baby."

"But she's going to be alright?"

"They think so."

Trevor breathed a sigh of relief but he was devastated for the Baileys over the loss of their child. No one loved children more than Isaiah and Brenda Bailey. And Shanice had been over the moon about having a little sister. The phone rang as he was contemplating what he should do about the current state of events. If he went to the authorities, there could be other members of the Bailey family targeted. If he told Isaiah what he knew, it would likewise put the rest of the family in danger.

Shanice picked up the phone. Trevor could tell by the conversation it was her father. "Well, Trevor's here right now." She adjusted the phone and addressed Trevor. "Dad wants to know if you would stay here with us until my grandma and grandpa can drive over from Sanford."

"Sure," Trevor said. He was happy to stay at the Baileys for now and help out. Although he wasn't supposed to be there at all since he'd spent months trying to convince Phil and his cohorts the Baileys weren't important to him.

A fat lot of good that had done him because, apparently, Phil had made good on his threats and Trevor knew why. He'd been giving them the runaround regarding expanding their operations to other states. Now it looked like he was going to have to relent and give them what they wanted.

Trevor hated how his stupidity had hurt the people he loved most, and the least he could do now was to console Shanice and her little brothers until Isaiah's parents came. He was in no hurry to get back to Phil's in his present state of mind anyway. His anger would only put himself and the Bailey family at further risk.

Chapter Twelve

Of course, Trevor's continued absence from the Baileys made them and Shanice suspicious and angry, in that order, especially after he went back to his plan of avoidance after the baby's funeral. Brenda and Isaiah called often, a conversation that would go something like:

"Hey Trevor, we're worried about you. Did we do anything to hurt your feelings? Or something?"

"No, I've just got a lot going on. You know, school, activities... and I've got a part time job now."

"Really? Where?"

He scrambled for a quick response that sounded credible, given the nature of his true *work*. If you could call it that. "Um, it's a work at home gig Uncle Phil got me. Nothing special, just a lot of busy work."

"Well, don't let it overwhelm you. We miss you, and we'd love to see you whenever you have time."

"I know, and I'll try to make it over sometime." Even as he said it, he knew he wouldn't. He wanted to steer Phil and his goons away from the Baileys as much as possible. Eventually, they stopped calling, but Shanice was another matter.

When Trevor refused Shanice's calls or wouldn't return them, she would just show up. One Saturday, she got on her bike and rode the seven miles to Philip's condo. Thankfully, she wasn't hurt on any of the several major streets she crossed to get there, and Philip was off to one of the casinos he frequented. Trevor answered the door expecting it to be either Frick or Frack checking up on him, which they did sometimes when Phil was out of town.

"What do you want ass—?" Trevor said, before he saw it was Shanice. He was going to say, "asswipe," But Shanice would've freaked out, so he was glad he was able to change what he was about to say, since it wasn't intended for her anyway. "—as I'm about to head out?"

Her face crumpled anyway, and it made him backpedal. "'Nice, I'm sorry. I don't have to leave right away." He opened the door a little wider and pulled her into the room so the neighbors wouldn't see a little girl crying on the doorstep.

He couldn't bear to see her cry, so he hugged her. "Shh, don't cry."

"Why don't you pick up the phone when I call, or come over to the house anymore?" she said through her sniffles.

Trevor took a deep breath. "Like I told you. It's just not a good idea for us to hang out anymore."

"But why?"

"Because, it's just not."

She stepped back, as her stubbornness emerged. "You can't even give me a good reason."

"I would if I could, Shanice. I promise. You don't understand what kind of pressure I'm in over here."

"Then you should at least tell my Dad so he can help you."

"And get taken from Phil and sent God knows where? No thanks." Although, that wasn't the truth either. If he made waves with the DCFS, or with Isaiah Bailey, he would be putting the Baileys at risk, especially Shanice. And if anything happened to her, it'd be lights out for him, too. He'd make sure of it.

"Is he out of town this weekend?" she said, looking around, as if she were almost fearful his Uncle Phil would come out any minute.

"Yeah."

"Then, why can't we hang out a while?"

Shanice looked so sad, and he didn't want to be the cause of her sadness. He caved. "Just for a little while, but I'm driving you back home."

"Mom and Dad say you haven't had your license long enough for me to ride with you."

"I think they'd rather I drove you than have you ride your bike back."

"Then I'll be busted."

"We'll figure it out," he said. "You had lunch yet?"

"No, I'm supposed to be at Carly's birthday party."

Trevor grinned. "What do you say, we order some pizza?"

"Okay!" Shanice said, then strode over and plopped down on the sofa in front of the TV. "I haven't had pizza in so long. Brenda cooks every day."

"And that's a problem, how?"

"It's not. I love Mom's cooking, I just want a Wendy's burger, or Papa John's pizza sometimes."

Trevor pulled out his cell phone. "I'm about to grant your wish, princess."

They scarfed down pizza and caught up. Shanice's twelfth birthday was rapidly approaching and Trevor's seventeenth, so a lot was going on with them both in school. He was gearing up for prom, and she was taking advanced math and science classes already. Trevor was impressed.

"How'd you land in pre-algebra anyhow? I didn't get any of that until 8th grade." Although he could've been in the more advanced classes earlier, it was David's desire to protect him that kept him back.

"They have this program for kids who think they might want to do something health-related, like nursing or medical school when they grow up."

"You want to be a doctor?" Trevor said.

"No, a nurse. I want to help people get over drug addiction and stuff, but I don't want to go to school for all the years it takes to be a doctor."

"That's cool. Just don't fall for some doctor and forget about me," he teased.

"I'd never forget you, Trevor," she said. "And I'll never fall for some doctor."

"How do you know?" he said. "You'll go off to college and I'll be as good as forgotten."

"You'll forget me first," she said. "You already have. You're the one who's taking Emily Winters to the prom and everything."

"It's just another rite of passage."

"A what?"

"It's one of those things you're expected to do at certain ages that transition you from one stage in life to another."

"Oh, well. I'm not passing any rites with anyone but you," She said.

"You're too young to say that, Shanice. You've got a lot of growing up to do."

"So do you." She protested, just as he expected her to.

"Yeah, but I'm closer to twenty-one than you are, and I'll be going off to college in a couple of years."

"I know, but I won't forget you," Shanice said with conviction.

"How do you know this?" Trevor asked.

"Because I'm going to be like Amy March in *Little Women*."

"Never heard of it," Trevor said.

"Probably because boys think it's stupid. But there is a *Little Men*, and *Jo's Boys* and they're about orphans and stuff. Anyway, they're classics. Mom read the books when she was about my age, so she gave them to me for Christmas."

"What does this have to do with you not forgetting me?"

"You'll have to read *Little Women* to find out," she said cryptically. Then she changed the subject by challenging him to a video game. About an hour later, Trevor drove Shanice as far as a block away from home, then took her bike out of his trunk so she could ride home the rest of the way.

"Hey 'Nice," he said. "Don't ride your bike over to Phil's again, or I'm going to snitch you out to Isaiah and Brenda. It's too dangerous for you to ride that far on your bike. You could get hit by a car."

She hung her head briefly, then raised her eyes to his again. "Then promise me you'll come see me sometimes."

"Okay," he said. "I promise." But Trevor knew the likelihood of him following up on that promise was practically nil.

He was finishing up another of Phil's projects before getting ready to go hang out with a couple of friends from school that night when he decided to look up *Little Women* on the internet. Trevor found a detailed enough summary to figure out that his surrogate little sister probably had a crush on him.

Trevor grinned, knowing that he would be one of many crushes before she finally decided on the man she would spend her life with. He wasn't even thinking of a future with any special person at the moment. He just needed to concentrate on figuring out how to get out of the mess he was in with his uncle Philip, and to keep Shanice and her family alive in the process.

·············●············

The drive to the University of South Florida was a short one from Orlando, and Trevor realized upon checking into his dorm that this was an experience most freshman shared with their parents. It was times like these that he really missed Elena and David. They would've been here, just like the many parents he saw accompanying their children to the dorms on their first day.

Trevor scolded himself and he hefted his belongings up to his room on his own. *Suck it up, Kyle. At least you're away from that asshole, Phil.*

For that he was grateful. He looked forward to not working for Phil anymore. For the first time he thought he might have a bright future. He'd get his degree in computer science and maybe found his own software startup company someday, and never go back to Phil and his fucked up life. Trevor was first to arrive so he got the choice side of the room, that is the side with the least worn furniture.

Even when everything was unpacked, his side looked sparse. He'd managed to cobble together most of what he needed from the lists the college provided, but as he watched his roommate settle

OBSIDIAN FAITH • 69

in with the help of his parents Trevor realized he'd missed some things. He was leaving his dorm to make a much-needed trip to Wal-Mart when a mini-van pulled up to the unloading area in front of his dorm, the horn blasting.

Isaiah, Brenda and Shanice hopped out. Trevor felt kind of shitty considering how he'd avoided them so much. Well, everyone but Shanice. She never stopped calling.

"What the... ?" Trevor said, not caring that his face-splitting grin wasn't how college freshmen trying to be cool behaved.

"We came to make sure you settled in okay," Brenda said. "We couldn't let our favorite new USF Bull move in without all the essentials."

"Yeah, and we brought you a lot of stuff, too," Shanice said, and sidled up to him. Trevor threw his arm around her shoulder and pulled her in close to his side, dropping a kiss on the top of her head.

He shared hugs all around with Brenda and Isaiah and then they brought the stuff they'd come with up to his room. Needless to say, a trip to Wally World wasn't warranted after the surprise shopping spree the Bailey's brought to him. Now he had a stocked mini-fridge, a microwave, and matching bed and window accessories.

"How'd you guys know I didn't have any of this stuff?" Trevor asked.

"Shanice told us you were driving down on your own," Isaiah said.

"And we knew Phil didn't have a clue," Brenda said. "Besides, we couldn't let Elena and David's only son go without a proper college send-off."

Trevor's throat tightened at the mention of Elena and David. He hugged Brenda, then changed the subject.

"So, where's Zeke and Ezra?"

"They're with grandma being spoiled to high heaven," Isaiah said.

Brenda popped her husband playfully on the back of the head. "My babies are not spoiled," she declared.

Isaiah bristled and backed away from his wife. "Actually, the boys are little angels," he said with an elaborate roll of his eyes.

"Well, they're not as spoiled as some of the other children at church, anyway." Shanice said.

Brenda smoothed the comforter on Trevor's bed one final time and stood back up. "Did we run your roommate and his parents off?"

"No," Trevor said, running a hand through his hair. "They went to dinner."

"Speaking of," Isaiah said. "We'd like to take you out to eat before we head back home, unless you've got other plans."

"Plans? What plans?" Trevor said grabbing his keys off his bedside table.

Dinner went by too fast for Trevor, but he wasn't about to be a wuss and beg the Baileys not to leave. They were just about the only people he'd miss in Orlando, to be honest.

When they dropped him off in front of the dorm they all got out again to say a proper goodbye.

Isaiah shook his hand and gave him a hug. "You have our numbers. If you need anything, don't hesitate to call."

"Thanks, Isaiah." Trevor said.

Brenda hugged him tight, tears threatening to spill from her eyes. "I'll send you care packages," she promised.

"Who does that anymore?" Isaiah said.

"I do," Brenda said with a stubborn hike of her chin. "My parents sent them to me when I was in college. There's nothing like getting little surprises in the mail."

"Thanks, Brenda." Trevor said. "I'll look forward to them."

Shanice clung to him and cried like she'd never see him again. "Aw, squirt," Trevor said, patting her back. "It's not the end of the world."

"It's just... I'm going to miss you so much."

"I'm going to miss you, too. But you can email or Skype me."

"And text and call sparingly," Brenda said. "Remember you just got that new cell phone for your birthday."

"Oh yeah," Shanice said, pulling away and rummaging through her little purse. "Here, put your number into my phone."

Trevor obliged her.

She grinned through her tears. "One for each other, and each other for one?"

"One for each other and each other for one." He recited it back and really meant it for the first time in a very long time.

Chapter Thirteen

While off at USF in Tampa, Trevor was just far enough away to have some freedom from his uncle. But that didn't stop Phil from calling and threatening the Baileys until Trevor agreed to do more work for him. The jobs got bigger and bigger, and the amounts ballooned.

Trevor thought he could immerse himself in college life and ignore Phil. He began to refuse to pick up when he called, and didn't respond to his emails or text messages. Maybe Phil would give up and wouldn't bother having him do his hacking projects anymore.

Was he wrong. Phil and his pet mobsters took the ride frequently to Tampa to submit their requests in person. They were on campus so much, they were on a first name basis with Trevor's friends. A fact that pissed Trevor off tremendously. The projects they had for him got more and more risky, more and more intricate, but Trevor had honed his skills even further now that he was getting a formal education as a computer programmer.

Trevor had almost completed his sophomore year when Phil hatched the plan that got Trevor in deeper with organized crime. His uncle actually showed up and dragged him out of class for that one.

As he followed Phil out of the computer lab to his car, Trevor saw they weren't actually going to Phil's car. There was a limousine idling at the curb in front of the building. As they approached, Frick got out and opened the door.

Phil scooted inside, but Trevor stood looking around, wondering if he should bolt. He figured they'd catch him anyway, and he was really not ready for a beat down, it being so close to finals and everything.

Trevor slid onto the leather seat between his uncle and Frack. On the other bench seat was the man he only knew as the Boss, who he'd met once when he began programming the slots for the guy. Frick got in and sat on the seat with the Boss.

"Hey kid," Frick said. "The Boss is about to make you an offer you can't refuse."

The Boss glared at Frick. "This is not The *Godfather*, asshole."

Frack and Phil laughed, but Trevor wasn't in the mood.

"Shut the fuck up," Frick said. Apparently the little guy didn't like being laughed at.

"All of you shut the fuck up," the Boss said, then addressed Trevor. "I'm sure this young man and I have better things to do than listen to you morons laughing it up."

"I was in a computer lab," Trevor said. "I need to get back so I can finish."

"We'll make this quick and painless," the Boss said. "I understand from Phil and my men that you have a unique skill which could make us all multi-millionaires, and I'm including you when I say all. How does that sound to you? It's Trevor, right?"

"I'm listening," Trevor said. He may be talking to the leader of the Orlando underworld, but he was not going to answer like a punk.

"We want to clean house. A one-time deal where we take as much of the unclaimed funds from each state as we dare, which Phil here estimates could be approximately one billion dollars. Split five ways, minus the money I'm willing to front you for equipment, that's a little less than two hundred million for each of us. Are you game, Trevor?"

Trevor knew from previous stories he overheard from Frick and Frack, the Boss was not someone to be trifled with. "Sure, but let me tell you, this is going to be a massive undertaking."

"Give that to us in man hours or something," Phil said. "Since this project is going to benefit you too, you might want to scrap school."

"That's... no way. I have to stay in school," Trevor said.

"You'll have so much money, kid, no one will look down on you not having a college degree," Frack said. "I don't got one, and look at me."

"Yeah, look at you," the Boss snarled. "A degree will help a man look legit when he's got to launder a large amount of cash. Trevor is right. He needs to stay in school."

Trevor breathed a sigh of relief when the Boss agreed with him, because he didn't know how he was going to get out of the mess they were trying to put him into just yet.

He answered the previous question posed to him by Phil. "It'll take a couple of years to make a program like that viable. Then it has to be tested, and troubleshooting sometimes takes longer than the programming. I can't work on it eight hours a day, but I can promise you I will work on it every day."

"That's all we can ask for," the Boss said. "I'll get whatever information you need from us when the time comes, but right now if you'll begin the process, Phil will help with the research. These two numbskulls will get to work on new identities for all of us and those significant others we want to take with us. You got anybody like that, Trevor?"

Trevor almost broke into a cold sweat, but he held it together. "No."

"You playing the field a little, eh? That's what a college boy should do. No need to tie yourself down until you're older," the Boss said.

"What about the Baileys?" Phil said. "Don't you want to include them in your outrageous fortune?"

"They don't mean shit to me," Trevor lied.

"Who do you think you're fooling? You know, that Shanice has gotten so fine, I wouldn't mind... " Trevor's fist connected with Phil's nose before he could finish his sentence, and then he pounced as blood dripped all over the front of his uncle's pricey suit. Frick pulled Trevor off while Frack grabbed Phil.

"She's a kid, you asshole!" Trevor screamed. Shanice was all of fourteen at the time, and Trevor had just intervened on her behalf the last time he'd been in Orlando when a boy who'd been obsessed with her since elementary school had begun to spread rumors about her. Owen Nettles had promptly forgotten Shanice's name after Trevor put the fear of God into him.

The Boss, who hadn't moved during the brief skirmish, glared at Phil. "We don't mess with kids, Kyle, and if I ever hear you have... " He left it there.

"So, Trevor Kyle, do we have a deal?" The Boss extended a hand for him to shake as if it were a foregone conclusion.

Trevor knew that it was, but he would play their game for now—as though he had a choice? He extended his hand.

"We have a deal."

Trevor all but stopped visiting or talking to the Baileys after that because he never knew if Phil and his henchmen were watching, and they'd already proven they would hurt them—or worse—if Trevor didn't do what they said.

Phil, pissed over Trevor embarrassing him in front of his mob friends, threatened Trevor until he extended their reach into North and South Carolina, where he funneled enough to keep Phil, Frick and Frack in gambling dough for several months at a time. If they ran low, they'd pay him another visit. Meanwhile, he was working on the program for the Boss which he'd dubbed The Grand Scam, and he'd also been thinking about how he could go about extricating himself from the deal.

In his senior year, Trevor began to leave little markers that he knew would eventually get him caught. He was tired of being a pawn. He figured he'd rather be the fed's prisoner than continue stealing for a cruel man who'd never been a father to him.

Chapter Fourteen

It was four months before his graduation when Shanice bummed a ride to USF with some girls who used fake IDs to get into frat parties. When she and her friends arrived at his frat house, the party had been in full swing. He'd been playing a game of beer pong with a few of his brothers, and they were scouring the floor for some girls to dance with.

"Hey, Trevor. Look at the hotties that just walked in the door," Bryce said. "Four of them. Four of us. Problem solved."

Bryce went over and pulled the exotic beauty Trevor had his eye on to the dance floor. Her coloring was similar to Shanice's, but she had a bod that couldn't possibly be attached to Shanice.

The last time he'd seen her it had been over Christmas break when he was a sophomore, and she'd still been as thin as a reed, with arms and legs too long to belong to such a tiny person. She'd been pissed at him, as usual, because he kept telling her it wasn't safe for her to come to his uncle's house, but she'd kept seeking him out, even though he'd told her they weren't brother and sister any more.

Then she giggled over something Bryce said, and he knew it was her. She was all grown up now. He walked out to the dance floor, where Bryce was grinding on her like a dog in heat, and grabbed her arm.

"Shanice?"

A crooked, sexy grin lit up her face, and she abandoned her dance partner. "Trevor!"

He scooped her up and she held onto him so tightly, Trevor hated himself for having disappointed her over and over again. When he finally eased her out of the embrace, he leaned over to talk into her ear over the music.

"What are you doing here?"

"Looking for you," she said. Then her beautiful face got serious. "You didn't come home for Christmas. What was that all about? I mean, I get you don't want to be my surrogate brother any more, but Isaiah, Brenda, and the twins, they still love you, too."

"Let's not do this here," he said. "Come on."

He led her through the throng of partiers and took the back stairs off the kitchen up to his room. Couples in various stages of making out occupied every spare corner in the house, a sight which usually didn't embarrass him, but it made him very uncomfortable with Shanice there. Of course, she was a different Shanice from the one he'd last seen, who could now put any of the college girls to shame.

He tried, unsuccessfully, not to look at her perfectly shaped ass as she walked ahead of him, or the tiny waistline just above it, or... . Finally, they got to his room and he let her in ahead of him.

The noise from the party was dulled but not totally gone. He grabbed a couple of water bottles out of his mini fridge, opened one, and handed it to her. Then he downed a huge swallow of his own. It was time to clear his head a bit for this conversation.

He gestured toward a chair, but she chose the bed, so he went to the chair.

"Do Isaiah and Brenda know you're here?"

"What do you think?" she said. "You leave me no choice but to sneak off to see you when I can, because you never come see us anymore. Why is that?"

It broke his heart to say the words, but he gave her the same bullshit answer he'd given her the year after Dave and Elena died. "I've grown up. We've grown apart. There's no blood connecting us, Shanice. You need to live your life and forget about me."

Her eyes filled and tears spilled down her face.

"What happened to us being the two musketeers? One for each other and each other for one?" They'd put their own spin on the musketeer phrase when they'd first moved to Orlando and lived on the same street. With their adoptive families so wound together and going to the same church, they'd believed they would be together forever.

"That changed when Philip Kyle got custody of me. Now you need to go back home, before you get into trouble here."

"I won't get into any trouble with you looking out for me. Besides, we just got here, and my friends aren't ready to go." She wiped her eyes with the back of one hand. "It's okay if you don't want to see me. I'll just go downstairs and dance with some of your hot college friends until my friends are ready to go. We can act like perfect strangers if that's what you want, but I'm not leaving right now."

With that, she stood and stalked over to his door. He rushed over and barred her from leaving.

"Just stay in here and hang with me," he said. The only alternative he had was to unleash her among his horny frat brothers.

She smiled knowingly. He wasn't fooling her. "Sure," she said, like that had been her plan all along.

They played video games together like old times and talked until they were practically hoarse before she got a text from one of her friends asking where she was. They were going to take a cab to the hotel. She texted back and told them she'd meet up with them the next morning.

Trevor didn't think anything of it when he gave her a new pair of his pajamas to sleep in, and they tucked in for the night in his bed.

Morning was another thing. When he awoke with a stiffy crammed against her derrière, he was mortified and was certain she'd be traumatized by his body's involuntary reaction. He jerked away from her, almost falling off the bed. She turned to look at him, unfazed.

"Have a tic-tac, Trevor." She pushed one between his lips as he looked at her slack-jawed. Apparently, she'd been awake before him.

Trevor cowered underneath the comforter, bending his knees so she wouldn't see it tented by something else. He rolled the tic-tac around in his mouth before he spoke.

"Good morning. Sorry about that."

"I'm going to nursing school when I graduate. I've already taken college-level anatomy. I know all about natural bodily functions," she said with a smile that could only be characterized as naughty.

Trevor stood, careful to keep his back to her as he adjusted himself, conjuring up images to help him hurriedly deflate. When he turned to face her, Shanice covered her face with the pillow and laughed.

"What's so funny?" Trevor wasn't sure if he should laugh with her, and therefore at himself.

She moved the pillow. "Whatever you just did, didn't help."

He looked down, and sure enough, he was at half-mast. She collapsed into a fit of giggles. Again. That did help. There is nothing like being laughed at by a girl to calm an overactive libido.

Trevor picked up his pillow ostensibly to cover himself, then thought better of it and threw it at her. Shanice tried to dodge it and fell off the bed. The force of her landing knocked the wind out of her mid-laugh. Concerned, Trevor ran around to the other side of the bed and helped her up off the floor.

"Are you okay?" His voice came out husky, when he realized his body was flush with hers. She looked both adorable and sexy grinning up at him. Despite his desire to continue to think of her only as his surrogate sister, Trevor felt an undeniable attraction.

Shanice threw her arms around his neck and went onto her tiptoes. He bent his head to lessen their height differential, meeting her soft, rosy lips for the first time. Just as her tongue tentatively touched his, he pulled away, swallowing his tic tac in the process.

"Trevor... " She moved back into his arms, wrapping hers around his waist. "We're not really sister and brother, you know."

"I know that." He peeled her arms from around him, and stepped back, because his dick was getting confused, and that wasn't a good look on him. Not in front of Shanice. Besides he'd promised Isaiah he wouldn't return his daughter's affections while she was still under the age of eighteen. "But we shouldn't be doing *any* of this."

He put some distance between them. "Let's get dressed so I can take you to breakfast."

Shanice sat back down on his bed, pouting visibly. He didn't like that he'd had to reject her, but it was the best thing all around, considering how he was still under Phil's thumb and if his uncle or

Frick and Frack got wind of her being there, her family could still be in danger.

He went into his bathroom and hopped into the shower. After he'd cleaned himself thoroughly, he turned the water to cold, hoping it would help keep him from reacting to Shanice, the girl he'd always loved like a sister, who was now very much a woman.

Chapter Fifteen

"Want my bacon?" Trevor remembered how much Shanice loved bacon for as far back as those early days in the group home when she'd bartered with him for his bacon.

Her amber eyes were sullen. "No thanks."

Trevor sighed. "'Nice, you know Isaiah would throttle us both if we let anything happen between us right now."

Something in his words must have given her hope because she smiled. "I know, right?"

"What's your Dad got, thirty pounds on me? I'm not trying to fight Papa Bailey right now."

"He'd definitely kick your ass," she said, taking a slice of the bacon he'd offered earlier. "But I'd like to think that I'm worth a good ass-kicking." She bit down on the crisp bacon and chewed.

Trevor tried not to become mesmerized by her lips. He took a drink of coffee. "You're worth a dozen or more good ass-kickings, but I want to finish college and you need to get into college, then maybe we can go out on a date, or something."

"Really?"

He smiled. "Really. But you have a few more rites of passage to experience and I've got to take the IT industry by storm and build something so I can provide for a woman like you."

Shanice grew serious. "I've always loved you, Trevor, but I've been in love with you since that time you were about to kick Owen Nettles' ass for spreading rumors about me."

"You don't know that, yet, Shanice. We've never had that kind of relationship, and it was never possible for me before now. That would've made me a serious pervert."

"Do you know that in the old days, girls got married at thirteen?"

"Yeah, I think I paid enough attention in grade school to remember something like that."

"And Amy March was about the age I am when she fell in love with Laurie."

"So, you think I'm your Laurie?" Trevor said with a smirk.

"I know you're my Laurie."

That was the last time Trevor saw Shanice before he was arrested on the eve of his graduation.

· · · · · · · · ·●· · · · · · · · · ·

Trevor decided that getting arrested was the most surreal experience ever, especially if you are a college student so close to graduation you can taste it.

When he began baiting the feds with his hacks, he assumed they would act slowly, like most people, including his uncle, said they did things. He'd hacked into the FBI's database and he knew they were on to him, so he decided to run the program the week of graduation, thinking they'd probably not pick him up until sometime after he had his diploma in hand.

The funneling would proceed slowly for seventy-two hours, then it would ramp up and take the balance of what he'd targeted from each state at once and hide it in the various overseas accounts he'd selected. Then he'd conveniently get arrested before he could divide it with his partners. This was his grand plan. He wanted the FBI to arrest him so Phil and the mob couldn't touch the money, and couldn't touch the Baileys, otherwise they'd never get the money. Then he'd have to win the trust of the feds to get them all out of the mess he'd gotten them into.

Trevor was sleeping off a bender when federal agents swarmed his frat house. He woke up from the gentle nuzzling of an assault rifle against the back of his head.

Two agents in assault gear yanked him up off the bed by and he stood before them in his boxers, hands behind his head just as they'd posed him while they read him his rights. He didn't know what possessed him, but he decided to goad them a little.

"Geez, how many feds does it take to arrest an unarmed college student the day before his graduation?" Trevor said to the only suit in the room, who happened to be a tall African American man who looked uncannily like Will Smith in the Mohammed Ali film.

The movie star look-alike answered him without missing a beat. "Every fucking one of us." Then punched Trevor's lights out.

When Trevor recovered, he was in what he could only describe as an interrogation room. His head lay on a table with drool running out the side of his mouth. When he sat up and wiped his mouth with the back of his left hand, he saw that the table was bolted to the floor, and there were two hard plastic chairs, one in which he was seated. His right hand was cuffed to one of the table legs.

The Will Smith wannabe entered the room carrying two coffees.

"I'm Special Agent Hemphill. You look like you could use one of these." He set one of the coffee cups in front of Trevor and kept the other one for himself, then moved to sit down on the other side of the table. The folder he carried in nestled under the crook of his arm was now splayed in front of him.

"You've been a bad boy, Trevor Landon Kyle." The dude even talked like Will Smith from Bad Boys.

"In what manner, Special Agent Hemphill?" Trevor said, playing dumb.

"Listen, cut the shit. I know and you know what you've been up to. You've been funneling money from the coffers of state unclaimed property funds to overseas banks."

Trevor looked affronted. "Who, me?"

Hemphill hit the table and Trevor flinched in spite of himself. This is what he had wanted, just not the day before he was to graduate, and now that he was in the hands of the feds and wasn't going anywhere before they got his story, he decided he might as well cooperate.

"Okay, okay. You've got me. I've been a bad boy and now it's time for the U.S. Government to punish me. I confess. I, Trevor Landon Kyle, am guilty of funneling millions of dollars from state unclaimed property funds, and I'm not certain I know how to retrieve it."

"What do you mean, you're not certain? It's a simple matter of reversing your program right?"

"Well, not really. I'd have to have access to a computer to write a program to override my original one, which I might add, took me years to perfect."

"You're shitting me, Kyle."

"I shit you not, Agent Hemphill. It's going to take years to back out of the code and find the fifty random passwords to reverse the program and restore the funds to the fifty states they came from."

"I'll arrange to get you computer time wherever you land, but in the meantime, we're going to turn you over to the U.S. Attorney's office so they can try your ass."

Oddly, Trevor breathed a sigh of relief when he heard these words. They processed him into the federal holding center to await trial. Two weeks into his stay, Trevor got a visit from Isaiah Bailey who, through his network of prison ministers, called in a favor to visit him.

The guy was in tears when they ushered Trevor into the private visiting room. Isaiah grabbed him and gave him the biggest bear hug ever, sobbing so hard, Trevor couldn't stop a few tears from falling from his own eyes as well. When Isaiah pulled himself together, they sat across from one another at a table much like the one that had been in the interrogation room at the holding center.

"Trev, man. Tell me you didn't do this."

Isaiah's pain was so palpable, Trevor wanted to break down and tell him the truth, but if he did, Isaiah would confront Philip and the connections Phil had with the mob would put Isaiah and his family in jeopardy. Trevor couldn't have that. Shanice was part of that family and he would protect them with his life, even if it meant losing his freedom for a while.

"I can't say that, Isaiah. I did this. No one else was involved."

Isaiah's brow furrowed. "I know Phil gambled a lot. Are you sure he didn't put you up to this?"

Trevor swallowed and lied again to Isaiah's face. "No, Philip was too busy gambling to monitor my activities. After David died, I continued to hone my hacking skills and I rummaged through some of Philips work papers and found out about the unclaimed property funds each state held. Then I figured out how to cover my tracks, but I guess I didn't cover them well enough. The feds have been monitoring my activities for a couple of years. Then finally before the day of my graduation, they had enough to arrest me."

"Trevor, you're going to go to prison for this. You can't steal that much money, which you've refused to restore, and expect them to give you probation. Can't you do your hacking magic and restore the money?"

"No. It's going to take several years to do that."

"You know this has devastated Shanice. Nothing Brenda or I have said or done has consoled her. You've got to give her some closure. Since you seem so hell-bent on throwing your life away, don't let her throw away hers. She was in line for valedictory honors, but your mess has her grades slipping, and she's moping around the house."

"I'm locked up, Isaiah. What do you want me to do?"

"Release her from the hope that there will ever be anything between you."

Isaiah's words shredded his heart, but Trevor held his face impassive as he responded to the pastor's request. "Okay."

Chapter Sixteen

"Trevor! Oh my God, Trevor, tell me this is some case of mistaken identity. You didn't really take that money. Did you?"

Trevor was elated to hear Shanice's voice over the phone, even though she was clearly in some distress over what he'd done, but he couldn't reassure her otherwise. He also could not go easy on her. Isaiah wanted a clean break so she could have a chance at a normal life—without Trevor in it.

That was a tall order, but Trevor would deliver, because the alternative was seven years of heartache for her.

"Trevor?"

"Hello, Shanice." He knew his response was lame, but he wasn't ready to let go right off the bat.

"You've been in jail over a month and the first thing you say to me is 'Hello, Shanice,' like nothing's happened?"

"I was doing this for us. Two orphans who got screwed over by the system. Don't you see? I thought I was smart enough I'd never get caught, but I messed up, okay?"

"Are you even listening to yourself, Trevor? You make it sound like we're victims, but we stopped being victims the moment we were both adopted by loving families."

"My loving family died, remember. I had Philip Kyle as a foster parent for three years."

"Okay, living with Phil hasn't been a cakewalk, but you were still cared for by us. The years you had with David and Elena had to have made some impact on your life. This isn't what they taught you. All this comes from Phil's influence, doesn't it?"

"That's just it, Shanice. You had the cakewalk. I had a nightmare."

"Then why didn't you let my Dad help you? They asked you so many times about Phil, but you made it seem like everything was okay."

"Well, that's neither here nor there, now. I've done this and now I have to pay my debt to society."

"But if you were coerced by Phil, the lawyers can help you."

"It doesn't work like that, Shanice. I'm not a minor and I've confessed. Phil didn't write the programs, or move the funds. I did that. Now I have to pay for what I've done."

"Trevor... " She sniffed, and that gave away that she was crying.

"Shanice, you have to go on with your life."

"No."

"Yes. You have to live like you never knew me, because I'm going to be here awhile."

"I'll wait for you."

"No, you won't. If you care about me, you'll do this for me."

"No, Trevor. I love you, I can't let you go through this alone. One for each other and each other for one... right?"

"No, Shanice. That was a dream. A fantasy created by two poor little orphan kids who've now grown out of it. This is the real world now, and you and I have to live in it."

"Trevor, please." She said this through a gut wrenching sob.

"It's for your own good. You have a bright future ahead of you. Don't snuff it out for a convict."

"You are not a convict and I'll never think of you that way."

"Yes, I am, and I have the number to prove it. You have a chance to graduate with honors and be that nurse you've always wanted to be. Take it."

"Trevor, I'll never give up on you." Shanice was sobbing openly now.

"I have faith that you will be the man David and Elena hoped to raise."

Trevor had to say the words that would give her the clean break Isaiah wanted. "Then you're the only one."

· · · · · · · · ● · · · · · · · · · ·

Shanice proved to be as stubborn as she was beautiful. She had gotten under his skin so long ago he couldn't exorcise her from his brain or his heart even if he wanted to. Now she was chipping away at his resolve through letters. Although he never wrote her back, Trevor got a letter from Shanice almost every week until about a month before he was tried and shipped off to his destination. By then he was so smitten there was nothing he could do about it.

Eighteen months after that heartbreaking conversation with Shanice by phone, Trevor was transported to the federal prison at Victorville, California. The terrain surrounding the facility looked nothing like Trevor was used to in Florida, where there was lush vegetation and lots of green space. The area surrounding the complex was mostly asphalt, concrete and gravel. The trees and greenery that made up the landscape dotted the area like sad punctuation marks.

Trevor didn't know a single soul when he arrived, except one. The first day, Trevor was escorted to meet the FBI agent assigned to his case.

"Hello, Kyle." Special Agent Donald Hemphill in the flesh greeted him.

Trevor was oddly happy to see the agent, but he wouldn't dare let him know this. "How'd you pull this off? I thought I was going to get to start fresh with a new suit."

"It's called a transfer, inmate. Sort of what you just experienced, except I get paid to do it as a free man. Unfortunately, you don't."

Trevor pulled out a chair and plopped into it.

Hemphill's eyes blazed in a glare that might scare a lesser man. "Did I say you could sit?"

"I figured I'd save you the trouble," Trevor said. No sooner had the words left his lips than he found himself jacked up against the wall. The agent was surprisingly strong even though he was about the same height and build as Trevor.

Hemphill's nose was centimeters from Trevor's as he spoke. "Listen, Kyle. I don't have time to play games with you. I'm here for one reason and one reason only. That's to retrieve the billion dollars you stole from the fifty state government coffers you saw fit for rob for your own perverse pleasure. I am not your friend or your goddamn babysitter, and the sooner you get that through your thick skull, the better."

Trevor didn't know why he pushed Hemphill the way he did. Maybe it was because he felt completely alone for the first time in his life. He'd finally pushed Shanice away, or that's what he currently believed, because he'd not gotten a letter from her in about a month.

Isaiah and Brenda didn't write, but they made sure he had money in his commissary account, and would send holiday cards with their ministry newsletters attached, giving him updates on them and their family. Sometimes there were also pictures of their children, and this included the woman he loved more every time he read her letters and saw an updated photo of her.

Trevor raised his hands in an act of surrender. "Okay, okay."

Donald let him go and took a seat. "Now sit down and let's talk man to man."

It was no surprise to Trevor that they first discussed another deal. If he was able to retrieve the funds in three months, the agency was willing to give him an early audience with the Probation Board, and to sweeten the deal, they would consider restoring his civil rights.

Trevor knew three months would only put him on the streets again only to put the Bailey family in danger, and he'd be manipulated by Phil and his mob connections to help them get the money. Then they would disappear to some country where they couldn't be extradited back to the United States, and he'd be left holding the bag. Literally.

Trevor's only option was to stay in prison until he devised a plan that worked to trap Phil and his co-conspirators, and to safeguard the Baileys and secure his freedom. Until that time, he would have to bullshit Special Agent Hemphill enough to keep him interested until the right opportunity presented itself.

"It's impossible, I can't override the program in three months, but I can write a new program."

Hemphill nodded. "What timeframe are we talking?"

"With a couple hours of computer time a day only, I'm guessing five years."

"Five years?"

"And that's the most conservative estimate. That's not taking into consideration testing time, and reworking if the tests fail."

"We only have the manpower to allow you two hours of computer time a day, Kyle. The FBI has other important cases to work on besides yours."

"I know, which is why I'm trying to be straight with you about how long it's going to take."

"You created the program that took the funds in two years."

"And I had more computer time after classes, in the middle of the night when I couldn't sleep, or was just plain bored."

"If that's what we have to work with, then I suppose that's what we have to work with." Hemphill stood. "We'll start tomorrow."

Chapter Seventeen

"Kyle, you've got a visitor."

Trevor had been at Victorville over a year before he heard those words. He was giddy with anticipation, because he purposely didn't try to make any real friends in the joint. He figured he'd learned enough bad habits from his Uncle Phil and his associates to last a lifetime. He didn't need any more.

The officer led him through the labyrinthine hallways until they came to the visiting area, a place he'd yet to spend any quality time since he'd been incarcerated. Other than Isaiah Bailey when he'd been in Florida, he'd had no other visitors.

Because she was a minor at the time he was convicted, Shanice wasn't allowed to visit him without parental permission. And knowing Brenda and Isaiah the way he did, he knew they wouldn't have allowed her to visit, partly because they didn't want her exposed to the prison experience, and neither did he.

When they entered the visiting area, Trevor swept the room looking for someone, anyone he might recognize. No one fit the bill particularly, but then something looked familiar about the petite, exotic beauty in the corner who suddenly came barreling toward him.

"Ma'am, no physical contact... " the officer escorting Trevor began, but her arms were around him, and her scent invaded his nostrils before the officer could step between them. Trevor fought back tears as he held Shanice in his arms, an experience that he'd only gotten to emulate in his dreams since he'd been incarcerated.

"Trevor, it's been too long." Shanice stepped back only when she got good and ready to, swiped under both eyes with her fingers, then addressed the officer. "Sorry, officer. I just haven't seen him in three years."

"First warning. Any further infractions and your visiting privileges will be terminated today."

The officer got them settled at the table in the corner where Shanice had been sitting when they came in and went back to his post.

Trevor was full to overflowing, and this visit meant the world to him, but he couldn't allow it to continue, no matter how desperately he wanted to. Since she was there, he would allow this visit, but there would be no more if he could help it. Trevor didn't know how far Phil's mob friends' influence went, but he wasn't willing to find out.

"What are you doing here, Shanice?" He asked in as neutral a tone as possible.

She folded her arms. "Good to see you, too, Trevor." Her voice was dripping with sarcasm.

Even annoyed, she was beautiful, and Trevor lost the stoicism and chuckled. "You are amazing."

"I know, right? I was wondering when you would finally acknowledge this."

"Cocky, too. What happened to the little girl who idolized me most of her life?"

"She grew up. The better question is what happened to the handsome nerd with the heart of gold, and how did he end up here?"

"That's so much water under the bridge, 'Nice. I accepted that when the U.S. Attorney's office accepted my plea."

"Fair enough."

"So, what brings you to sunny California?"

"Didn't you get my last letter before they shipped you off, and the graduation pictures I sent you?"

"No, I didn't. The last letter I got from you was in April of last year. They moved me here at the end of April, and all I've gotten since I've been here are Isaiah and Brenda's holiday cards and newsletters with personal notes every once in a while."

"I'm a student at Stanford."

Trevor's jaw dropped. "You're in Silicon Valley, Santa Clara County?"

She nodded. "Yep."

"Wow! Shanice, that's ... I knew you were in college, but I didn't know it was such a good school, and that you were so ... close."

She frowned. "If you call six hours away close."

His eyes grew wide. "You drove six hours alone?"

"No, a friend and I flew to LA together, and I drove a rental here."

"You and a friend?"

He didn't ask the obvious, but she rolled her eyes and answered anyway. "It was a girlfriend. Lisa."

Trevor decided to change the subject, since he'd been so blatant about the identity of her friend. "So, how'd you end up at Stanford? I thought you were looking at Florida schools."

She smirked. "I was, until this idiot I know stole a billion dollars from all fifty states of the union."

He laughed and she joined him. "So, you've been at Stanford since last August?"

"Yeah. I had to get a handle on my studies and it took a while to trust anyone I knew with your story, because Mom and Dad didn't want me to make the trip alone."

Trevor loved Isaiah and Brenda for being such caring parents for Shanice. "They're right. Coming alone would be a bad idea. In fact, coming at all is a bad idea."

"I did not come to school in the same state as you to be told I can't come visit."

"I know, but you're here to get an education, not visit a convict every weekend."

"Well, I couldn't come every weekend anyway, but maybe once a month or so."

"Not even that much. Listen, as much as I appreciate your visit today, you can't come here again."

"Why?"

"Because there's really no point."

"No point? Didn't you read my letters? I meant it when I said I would never give up on you, Trevor."

"Visiting me could get you hurt."

"I don't care about that."

"Well I do!" Trevor's raised voice caught the attention of just about everyone in the room, so he toned it down. "Shanice, what I did pissed off some very bad people."

"Is your Uncle Phil one of those people?"

"That's beside the point."

"No, it isn't. You can't convince me that Philip Kyle didn't play a part in you landing in jail. Mom and Dad believe that, too. We just don't have any proof."

"And you don't need any. I'm here, paying for what *I* did. I wish the people who want this money didn't know how much your family means to me, but they do. Do you want your parents or the twins to be hurt?"

"What do you mean?"

"These people wouldn't hesitate to use you and your family to get to me. I spent the last couple of years I was in college trying to distance myself from you guys."

"But I kept pushing the issue," Shanice said, realization suddenly dawning on her. "Was Mom's accident caused by these bad people?"

Trevor nodded, his expression grave. He couldn't bring himself to say the words.

Fresh tears sprung into Shanice's eyes. "I lost my baby sister because... I knew there had to be a reason you kept pushing us away."

"Believe me when I say, I would have sacrificed myself in her place if I could have. I was so stupid in the beginning. I was a dumb kid thinking I was paying my keep. Helping out. Then they asked for more and more, until it wasn't just Florida stuff anymore. Those men who shadow Phil are no joke. I had to put myself in a place where they couldn't touch me, and by default couldn't touch you or your family until I could figure out a way to keep us all protected."

"Have you figured it out yet?"

"I'm working on it, but honestly, Shanice, it could be years before that happens. I have to get the feds to trust me, then I'll be hoping they will be willing to reward that trust with a deal that will bring the others to justice, while keeping you and your family out of harm's way."

"I know you can do this, and I'll wait for you. As long as it takes."

Trevor is shaking his head before she can finish her pronouncement. "No."

"What do you mean, no?"

"You can't wait for me. You need to live your life. You need to forget about me, because it's not a given that I'm going to come out of this anytime soon. I can't ask you to do that."

"You're not asking me. I said I was, and I am."

Trevor remembered his promise to Isaiah. "No, Shanice."

She implored him with her eyes. "Listen to me, Trevor. I love you, and I will always love you."

"I have three more years and some change in here. There's a lot of living you can do in three years. Don't let my situation stop you."

"I won't." Shanice sighed. "Listen, do these bad people have access to your mail?"

"Not that I'm aware of."

"Well, if it's too dangerous and I can't visit you, I'll write you, and you have to promise to write me back."

Shanice had sufficiently worn him down, so Trevor succumbed. "Okay, but we shouldn't save the letters... destroy the paper trail."

"Okay," Shanice said with the biggest grin since they'd sat across from one another. "I have faith in you, Trevor Landon Kyle."

"What is faith, anyway? It must be blind or stupid to believe in a fuck up like me."

"My Dad says faith is the substance of things hoped for, the evidence of things not seen."

"That sounds about right, because I don't know how you see any in me. I've done horrible things—things that make me undeserving of a preacher's daughter."

"There's nothing you can do to sway my faith in you. I have loved you since I was five years old and I know you've loved me, too. Maybe not in the way I wanted you to when I was eleven and trying to be the Amy to your Laurie, but I believe with all my heart we're destined to be together, so you might as well accept it, Trevor Kyle."

Trevor felt so bound by his promise to Isaiah, he still couldn't give her the three little words she craved, but he felt them. Trevor felt them with all his heart.

Chapter Eighteen

Shanice's first letter ripped his heart out of his chest and he bawled like a baby.

Dear Trevor:

We have loved one another like siblings most of our lives. It is now time for us to come to know one another as best friends, future lovers, and confidantes.

The background we come from does not lend itself to being open, honest, and depending on another person—one can only trust oneself. Our biological mothers didn't have our backs and that scarred us. My parents sent me to therapy for years, and they showed me so much unconditional love, I am mostly healed of those scars. You, however, lost David and Elena when you needed them most, so your path to healing was interrupted, and Philip did not to help you continue on that path.

I remember Phil having lots of parties and I'm sure you were exposed to many things my parents shielded me from. I remember catching you smoking pot with those boys, and you going to prom with the girl with the worst reputation at our little Christian school. You mentioned having done many other things you're not proud of, and I know you couldn't resist the temptation that Philip's upbringing, or lack thereof, afforded you.

I was serious when I said that nothing you've done could sway my faith in you, nor kill the love I have for you. You are my destiny and I won't allow another few years in prison deter me from it.

Let me introduce you to your future: I'm Shanice Anderson Bailey, daughter of Isaiah and Brenda Bailey, sister of Ezekiel and Ezra Bailey. I am a nursing student at Stanford University. Purple is my favorite color. The Kings of Leon are my favorite band. I cry when I watch sappy romantic comedies. I read a book almost every week, simply because I love getting immersed into the lives of fictional characters. I love a man who has had my back since we were children, and I will never stop loving him.

Now I have to go study, but I will write again. Never fear that I won't.

Yours always and forever,

Shanice

Letter writing is one of those lost arts that Trevor had never mastered. In this digital era, all he wanted to do was email and text Shanice, but he knew those modes of contact could be easily scrutinized. However, he felt like by the time he got her letter, the immediacy of response was lost. Especially when she could be struggling with something, or needed his shoulder to lean on. Getting his response a week later just didn't cut it.

Donald Hemphill, of all people, gave him the answer to his dilemma.

"Your girl is in a college dormitory, right?"

"Yeah."

"You know those hall payphones, the landlines, they're available for use by everybody in the building, even though most students today have cell phones."

"Right."

"So, all you need is some money on your telephone card account, and you can call her on the payphone in her dorm."

"You're a genius, Hemphill."

"Tell me something I don't know."

"Man, I could kiss you!"

"You do, and you'll draw back a face with no lips."

"You've got a billion dollars to recover through me. You can't do that."

"You don't need lips to write code."

"Oh, right."

"Speaking of which. Get back to it, dude. I'm outta here in thirty minutes, and like I've told you a million times. You are not my only case."

· · · · · ●●●●● ● ●●●●● · · · ·

Trevor Landon Kyle /05555-055
FCI VICTORVILLE
FEDERAL CORRECTIONAL INSTITUTION
P.O. BOX 5555
VICTORVILLE, CA 61555

June 30, 2010

Dear Shanice:

You may not have Isaiah and Brenda Bailey's blood, but you're certainly their daughter! For the first two years I was locked up, your letters were my lifeline, my grip on reality, my only hope in this seemingly hopeless place. But it was your visit last week that finally convinced me your unwavering faith in me is not misplaced. I'm willing to accept it, because as you said, "Faith is the substance of things hoped for, the evidence of things not seen."

You put your complete trust and confidence in me the first day we met, but I've held myself away from you, because everyone else in my life left me. I couldn't wrap my head around the idea that you would never forsake me until last week. For a little woman, you're certainly not a pushover. You say I'm the one who schooled you, but I can't remember being as strong for you as you've been for me over the years.

From this day forward, I'm yours in good times and bad, forever and always. What I hate now more than pushing you away after David and Elena died, or pushing you away again before I came here, was not realizing my mistake and acting on it while you were here. Thank God you didn't take my irrational doubts to heart.

Since we were children, I've hoped for so much for both of us, despite my life taking tragic turn after turn. I'm so happy the Baileys were able to give you the stability you deserved. I can only hope when I'm released, we can take the time to build the kind of life we've always longed for... together.

I love you so much, Shanice. I'm sorry I didn't say it while you were here in front of me, and I promise when I get out of here, I will not fail to say it, or to show it to you every day of our lives.

Eternally yours,

Trevor

P.S. - Please send me the phone number for the payphone on your dormitory hall.

Trevor couldn't say that his time flew by, but it did go better now that he was back in contact with Shanice again. They still wrote letters, but he lived for the times when they had phone conversations. Their unorthodox courtship wasn't what he would've wanted for her, but anytime he tried to apologize for it, she scolded him.

"Shut it, Trevor! Don't you dare try and insinuate that you're not good enough for me."

"It's true. You deserve so much better, Shanice."

Her voice became infinitely softer. "Baby, listen to me. You did what you had to do to keep us all alive. That makes you a hero in my book."

"What book are you reading, girl? One where the villain becomes the hero?" He hoped his teasing would lighten the heaviness he'd just dropped on her.

"One where the hero has a dark past with an evil uncle, but he thwarts the evil uncle's plans and his character arc makes a complete one-eighty. Then the hero and the heroine live happily ever after."

"I need to start reading from that book then, huh?"

Her response was always definitive. "Yes, you do."

Their conversations and her letters are what kept him going. They talked about just about everything, and they came to know one another on the most intimate level possible emotionally. Physically would have to wait until he was free man. Shanice sometimes tried to engage him in more intimate conversations by phone, but he squashed that idea fast.

"I don't need that. You know this, right?"

"I thought maybe since we can't be together in the flesh, it's something I can do to take the pressure off," She said.

He insisted. "That's not necessary."

"So, you've given up on sex?"

"No. I didn't say that."

"Then what are you saying?"

It was so like his girl to push the envelope. Trevor was so proud to be able to call her that and so lucky to have her even though he was in this reprehensible place. "Shanice, I don't want to ever treat you like these guys in here treat their women. Before you know it, I'll be out of here. Then we can get married and do things the right way."

He could her audible gasp. "You want to marry me?"

"Well, yeah, that's the plan."

"When were you going to clue me in to this plan of yours if I hadn't asked you all these other questions?"

"Well, I wanted to wait until I was out of here, so I could do it at a restaurant or something, but you're pushy."

"Who are you calling pushy, Mister?"

"Shanice Anderson Bailey is who."

She huffed. "If you weren't where you are and you had the ability to call me right back, I'd hang up on you."

"How do you know I'd call you right back?"

"Because you love me," she said simply.

"Well, that's true, but maybe I'd want to teach you a lesson and not call you right back."

"As if!"

"Watch me. Goodbye Shanice... ."

"Trevor, if you hang us this phone... ."

"You'll what?"

"Ooh, you make me want to strangle you."

"But in a good way, right?"

"Look who's talking dirty now?"

"I didn't mean it in a dirty way. I—"

"You what?"

He conceded defeat. "You win, Babe. I've got nothing."

"Are you going to always let me win when we fight."

"When we fight? You say it as if you expect it."

"Even happily married couples fight, Trevor. My Mom and Dad did all the time."

He whined in a say-it-ain't-so tone. "Not Pastor Isaiah and Brenda?"

"Like cat and dog when it was about something either one of them were passionate about."

"Like what?"

"Money, disciplining the boys or me, Dad saying something stupid. Oh, and money."

Trevor's heart sank. "Then we're doomed."

"Why do you say that?"

"When I get out of here, I'm going to be so broke I won't be able to pay attention."

"I'll be taking the nursing boards around the time you get out so we won't starve."

"Shanice, I'm supposed to take care of you."

"Where is that rule written?"

"It's man code."

"And who told you that?"

"Nobody. It's just hard-wired into most men's DNA to want to take care of his woman."

"That's stupid."

"Come again?"

"If there's one thing I learned living with my parents, it's this: gender roles are not static. When my parents got married, they both worked and took care of each other. Mom, didn't work when we moved to Orlando because it was cheaper to stay home and raise the boys daycare being what it was. Besides, Dad made enough to take care of all of us—most of the time. He's so generous he sometimes got into trouble financially because he was always bailing someone out of something. That's when they fell short and they'd fight over money. Mom went back to work when the boys went to middle school, so now they're taking care of each other again."

Trevor realized he was likely one of those people who made the Baileys fight over money. They'd stepped up to plate for him financially ever since he'd been incarcerated, and a few times even before that. He would just have to figure out a way to pull his weight legally when he got out.

"How'd you get so smart?" he asked.

"Book smart or common sense smart?"

"Both."

"I had a lot of time on my hands growing up, because I was infatuated with this boy who saved me from some bullies when I was five."

Trevor had to hurry up and get off the phone before the woman he loved heard him cry for the first time. He was so overcome with emotion he couldn't speak for a few seconds.

"Do you remember why you did that, Trevor? All these years and I've never thought to ask until now."

Trevor cleared his throat. He'd promised to be painfully honest with her, so he had to tell her. "My little sister, Natalie. You reminded me of her. Her death is what caused DCFS to take me into the system."

"Oh, Trevor, I'm so sorry."

"It's okay now. Her death likely saved us both from so much other shit my Mom would've undoubtedly dragged us into."

"The same with my mother's death. If she'd lived, who knows what I would have become."

"You're a fighter, 'Nice. You were always going to be all right."

"You, too, Baby. And it doesn't matter where you are now. You're going to be all right, too."

Trevor could only nod in agreement and hope his future bride was right, because currently, he had no clue how he was going to fix the mess he'd gotten them into. However, he went away from that conversation with a new resolve to make things right, and then figure out how to build a future for them.

PART TWO: The Evidence of Things Not Seen

Chapter Nineteen

June 27, 2014

Trevor Kyle shuffled in restraint chains to his exit interview with Special Agent Donald Hemphill. There was no eagerness on his part, even though he'd be free the following Monday. But he wouldn't miss the hand and leg jewelry.

The guard escorting him stopped at one of the holding cells that masqueraded as a lawyer/client meeting room, and opened the door. Hemphill sat in the hard plastic chair on the opposite side of a metal table. After his restraints were removed by the guard, Trevor took the chair opposite the agent who'd visited him frequently asking for favors since he'd been locked up. They were on a first-name basis, but Trevor addressed him formally when he was being sarcastic or needed to make a point.

"You don't look like a man who's getting out of this joint in a couple of days, Trevor," Hemphill said.

Truth be told, Trevor was not as happy as he should have been about leaving. Now he had no more leverage against the man who liked to call himself his foster father but who was nothing more than his legal guardian. He'd have to give Philip what he wanted or risk losing the only person who mattered to him in some horrific way he couldn't do a damn thing about.

"What do you want, Donald?"

Donald looked down at a lone manila folder sitting neatly in front of him. "I'm going to tell you what I've discovered in the last couple of weeks, and you're going to listen, so together we bring to justice the mastermind behind this crime for which you took the lone fall."

Hemphill had cajoled, threatened, manipulated, enticed, and used all kinds of persuasion he could in the seven years Trevor had been in prison to get him to tell him the location of more than one billion dollars he'd stolen by hacking into each state's unclaimed property accounts. Hemphill had also offered him deals to get him out of prison earlier, believing this would be the one incentive that would make Trevor talk, but he'd needed more. He'd made it clear there would have to be assurances made regarding the safety of Shanice Bailey and her family.

Trevor didn't dare get his hopes up. He knew if there was anyone who could get inside the criminal mind enough to catch an oily scumbag like his uncle, it was Special Agent Donald Hemphill.

"Show me what you've got," Trevor said. "Then I'll let you know if we can deal."

Hemphill smiled and pushed the folder toward him like he was moving a chess piece.

·········●·········

Within the hour after his exit interview, Trevor was out of his prison garb and wearing regular clothes for the first time in many years. It felt weird. He and Hemphill were making their way to Las Vegas, in what was undoubtedly a federal vehicle.

If he'd been smart enough to siphon off a few million of what his uncle had instructed him to steal, he would have had new identities and passports waiting for him and Shanice upon his release. They could've disappeared this weekend and not even have had to deal with his goddamned uncle at all. No one would have been able to find them, including the small cadre of federal agents Hemphill had working every angle.

Hindsight was twenty-twenty, of course, and additionally, if Trevor wanted to prove to Shanice he was indeed a better man than the federal government had proven him to be seven years ago, he needed to do it this way.

They were in the city limits of Las Vegas when Donald shared some pertinent information with him.

"Shanice Bailey is already here."

Trevor slipped his hand underneath Hemphill's tie and twisted. He tightened it like a noose around the agent's neck. "What the fuck kind of games are you playing, Hemphill?"

Hemphill gasped and pulled the car over. "Listen...What would you have done if you'd known a couple of hours ago? Agonized over it all the way here?" Trevor released loosened his grip but didn't remove his hand from the loop of the tie. Hemphill said, "She sweet-talked your release date out of your frazzled caseworker and came to surprise you. There was nothing we could've done to stop her, unless we'd gone in to talk to her without your knowledge. We wanted you to take this deal, not piss you off by talking to your girlfriend first."

"Where is she?" Trevor yelled.

Hemphill pried Trevor's hand away from his neck and shook him off. "Do that again, and our deal is off the goddamn table." He adjusted his tie and straightened himself out. "She's staying with a friend who graduated with her a couple of weeks ago. Apparently this girl's father is friends with the pastor."

Trevor shook his head. "Is there anything else you need to tell me before this shit goes down next week? I need to figure out how to get Shanice out of harm's way before I meet my dear old uncle Monday morning."

"We've got a room for you at the New York, New York Hotel. Our treat." Hemphill reached into his inside suit pocket and handed Trevor an envelope. "Here's a little pocket change to get you around while you handle your personal business. We'll touch base Sunday afternoon about the sting operation."

They rode in silence until he pulled into a gated community north of the Air Force base. "Call a cab or something when you get ready to check into the hotel. It wouldn't do to have me hanging around your girl and her friend looking like a federal agent."

Trevor sighed. "Look, Donald, I'm sorry. I'm not rational at all when it comes to Shanice, okay? You should've told me sooner. If you want my full cooperation, you need to keep her out of this as much as possible."

Hemphill waved him off. "We'll figure out together how to keep her out of Philip Kyle's crosshairs until we get him into custody. I'll see you tomorrow, ready to rock and roll."

"Thanks, man," Trevor said and opened the car door.

As Hemphill sped off, Trevor realized the bag containing all his worldly goods was still in the trunk. He could only hope someone would drop it off in that room the feds were paying for.

Chapter Twenty

Trevor went to the door and knocked. He was so nervous and wondered how Shanice would react. A girl he assumed was Shanice's friend answered the door.

"Yes?" she said.

He looked in and saw Shanice eating Doritos. When she looked up and saw Trevor, she dropped the bag and ran over it, and he could hear the remaining contents being crushed. She collided with Trevor on the stoop and jumped into his waiting arms. She wrapped her legs around his torso, and he hefted her into his arms. Tears rained down her cheeks as she bombarded him with sloppy kisses all over his face.

"Oh my God! Oh my God!" she reiterated like a mantra.

When their lips finally met, they latched on and didn't let go for an awkward amount of time.

"Um, you guys might want to get in here before those barking dogs bring the whole neighborhood out to watch you two make out on my doorstep," Lisa said.

They stopped kissing just long enough to notice Lisa, who stood with her arms folded, watching them in amazement. Shanice showered him with more kisses.

"Sorry," Trevor said. "Didn't mean to be rude." He closed the door and did a bow-legged walk toward Lisa, still carrying Shanice in his arms. Holding her carefully with one arm, he reached the other hand out to Lisa and introduced himself. "Trevor Kyle."

"I would certainly hope you're the Trevor she's bent my ear about for the past four years and not some random guy who showed up on my doorstep to make out with her."

Trevor laughed. "That's one thing I'll admit being guilty of."

"Make yourself at home," Lisa said. "I'm going into my room to watch some riveting Friday morning TV, unless you brought a sex-starved friend with you from prison who I can play with today." The girl had the nerve to look hopeful.

Shanice tore her lips away from him. "Lisa!" Then to Trevor, she said, "Remember how I told you she has no filter?"

"I'm beginning to see that firsthand," Trevor said. "And the answer is no. I tried not to make any friends while in prison. Sorry." His mind went to Donald Hemphill, the federal agent had been the closest thing he'd had to a friend while he'd been inside. He might have to ask the guy for another favor. Later.

"Too bad," Lisa said. "Hey, aren't you out early? I thought Shanice said you were getting out on Monday. We had the GPS ready to pick up your ass early Monday morning."

"Yeah, baby. How did you know I was here?" Trevor scrambled to think of an answer. He was grateful when Shanice said, "Oh, you called my parents."

"Something like that," he said.

Lisa backed towards the hallway, "Well, you kids catch up, fuck like a couple of bunnies, or make sweet love on my parents' couch. It's leather, so you won't leave stains like I did on their other sofa that one time when I was in high school."

Trevor shook his head, and Shanice grew almost purple with embarassment. When Lisa disappeared down the hall, they collapsed against each other and laughed.

Trevor said. "Where are her parents?"

"After our graduation, her father had to go out of the country on Air Force business and her mother went along. I've been here with Lisa for three days... waiting." Her amber eyes clouded up again, and her chin quivered. "And now you're here."

Trevor pulled her close into his arms and molded her to him. His body had yearned for this kind of closeness when she'd visited him the few times she'd been able to or on nights after he'd talked to her on the phone. Even when he read one of her letters. Now he had the woman he loved in his arms, and he never wanted to let her go.

Of course, he'd have to for however long it took for Hemphill and his team to get enough on his uncle to take him into custody. Trevor hoped like hell it would be as easy to get him to confess his part in the scheme, while simultaneously providing the other part of the code to retrieve the stolen funds.

His face grew warm when he realized he was sporting a boner the consistency of granite. He gently held Shanice away from his body, but she pressed back into him. "Sweetheart," he said sheepishly, "If you don't stop that I'm going to have a messy and embarassing situation on my hands."

"What?" she mumbled against his chest. "Oh!" She jumped back, but her focus was drawn to what was going on in his pants. He felt his face heat up even more, and he turned away from her to try and discreetly adjust himself, but his body wouldn't cooperate. Then he decided it might be better if he sat down, so he strode over to the couch, where Shanice promptly joined him.

"Don't worry about it," she said. "I'd be more worried if you didn't have that reaction to me after seven years."

"I know, but that's not all I want from you, Shanice. I love you, and I want us to do everything how Isaiah used to say, 'decently and in order.' Just like he did with your mother."

"But why?" Then her plea turned to resolve on a dime. "Trevor Kyle, I have done without you for seven years, except on paper and by telephone most of the time. I've been married to you in my heart since you admitted your feelings for me after three years of langishing in that prison, hoping we'd all forget about you. If you don't make love to me tonight, I'm going to explode!"

He became more and more shocked as she kept on talking. "What if it had been Monday when I'd gotten out?"

"Semantics," she said. "I promised myself you would make love to me on the day you got out of prison, and that day is today."

"What's the rush? The world isn't ending. After I've gotten on my feet, we'll get married in your father's church and have that honeymoon in Africa you've always wanted."

The tears came again and broke his heart. All he could do was look at her with all the love he had in him as she pleaded her case.

"You pushed me away, not once, but twice," she whispered through a pained voice that affected him almost as much as the first time he'd rescued her from the bullies. "I won't survive it again. I need to have something of you that will assure me you won't push me away again."

"If I took advantage of you like that, I'd be as dishonorable and untrustworthy as the monster my uncle made me."

"You are the honorable man my father and David Kyle created, not who your uncle tried to make you. So, no more waiting. I need you to make love to me, Trevor, because I need you to know from this day, not some arbitrary date in the future, we are one and we will never be separated again."

It was all he could do not to grant her wish. As much as he wanted to, he knew if he took her before they were married, he wouldn't be able to look his future father-in-law in the face. Long ago, when Isaiah came to terms with the way his daughter felt about Trevor, he'd exacted a promise from him, and as much as Shanice had tried to get him to break that promise even before he went to prison, he couldn't do it. He had only one alternative.

"Let's not wait, then." He paused for effect. "Marry me, tomorrow."

"Tomorrow?"

"Yes. We're in Vegas, the elopement capital of the world. There are little chapels all over this city," he looked at his watch. "Let's go get our paperwork done at City Hall."

She stood as if the action was her answer and gave him a level stare. "Let's go do this."

"Yeah?"

"But, before we go, I need you to ask me again, and this time do the down on one knee thing."

Trevor could only comply.

Chapter Twenty One

Special Agent Donald Hemphill took the stool next to Trevor at the hotel bar. Trevor was having a boilermaker. Hemphill flashed his credentials and waved the pretty blonde bartender away, but not before he gave her a broad smile and an "I'm your man if you want to get out of here later" wink.

Trevor glared at the FBI agent, who was almost as much of a chick magnet as James Bond, a fact he'd come to know in the almost eight years they'd known each other. At least once a year while Trevor had been imprisoned, Hemphill had collaborated with him on one case or another. "Last I checked, drinking wasn't on the list of no-no's for ex-cons."

"Maybe not, but I know from experience brides don't care much for sloppy-drunk grooms on their wedding nights. It dulls the performance."

Trevor did a double-take. "How'd you know about that?"

"Connections. I got the memo. And if I got the information this fast, what makes you think Phil won't? He has 'connections,' too."

"I don't care. With all that's going on, she's the one good thing in my life. I want to make her happy."

"But you're putting her in danger. He's threatened her to get to you."

Trevor shook his head. "I can take care of myself. And Shanice. I'm going to give her a honeymoon, too."

"Trevor," Hemphill said and sounded like he was trying to control himself. "Phillip could already be in town. You should be holed up in your hotel until we do this thing. I knew it was a mistake when you refused protective custody."

"I've been in prison for seven years. You guys standing guard while I sit in my room would be the same thing."

Hemphill put his hand on Trevor's arm. "But if something happens to you, our whole case falls apart."

"Isn't what you're doing considered harassment or something? I don't need babysitting. I'm a man of my word. I'm going to help you get Philip."

Hemphill narrowed his eyes. "I'm not so sure. Can you even think straight where Shanice Bailey is concerned?"

Trevor groaned and scrubbed his face. "I'm marrying Shanice tomorrow, whether you like it or not. Philip is a shifty bastard. He may get me to transfer that money and put a bullet in my head before you and your entourage get a chance to storm the room."

"You should have more faith in me, Trevor. Have I ever been bested by anyone other than you?"

Trevor knew Hemphill's record. He was good at catching the bad guys, which is why Trevor put his trust in the guy in the first place.

"Isn't there a first time for everything?" Trevor asked.

"Maybe a better question right now, is why are you drinking on what should be the happiest day of your life? From every indication, this is the girl who's stuck by you like Tammy Wynette. What gives?"

Either Hemphill was asking the right questions, or Trevor was ripe for spilling his guts. "Shanice has a nursing degree and a promising career ahead of her. What have I got? A felony charge and nothing substantive to offer her in the way of a secure future."

"Apparently, you didn't read the fine print, my friend. If we get enough to convict Philip, not only will we protect you and yours from any retaliation on his part, the federal government is prepared to offer you a job in our cybercrimes division once he's safely put away," Hemphill said.

"Will I have to move to Quantico?"

"Not necessarily. You can work mostly from home. We might need you to come in every once in a while and train the other agents in the division from time to time, but you and the new Mrs. can live wherever you want."

"That would be somewhere in Florida."

"So, you're going back home," Hemphill's tone indicated it was a statement, not a question.

"Yeah, I don't want to take Shanice far away from her parents, if I don't have to."

"Look at you. Already thinking like a husband and believing you'll survive your Uncle Philip."

"Just wait till I tell you what else I want."

"Okay, keep it down to something doable. Even I can't work miracles."

"I'm sure you can do this, even if you have to spot me until Uncle Sam gives my request a green light."

"You want an advance," Hemphill stated.

"It's not unreasonable. I have a wedding and a honeymoon to bankroll all of a sudden."

"This is true. You've likely earned every cent, given the help you've provided us the last seven years. I can go up to five figures without having to fleece my superiors."

"Cool. How soon can you get it?" Trevor asked.

"Give me a couple of hours."

"Banks are open here on the weekends?"

"Trevor, this is Sin City. Everything's open on the weekend."

· · · · · · ● · · · · · · · · ·

"Please recite the vows you have prepared for one another," the slight, balding minister said. Lisa, the maid of honor, wedding planner, and self-appointed amateur photographer, snapped pictures, while Donald, who'd been wrangled by Trevor into being the best man out of necessity, played videographer. He'd been worried about Lisa and Shanice catching on to who he was, but in the tux, he didn't look like a federal agent.

The Burning Love Wedding Chapel was the first one they found that resembled her father's church. If they were going to do the Vegas thing, they'd wanted it to look more like a sacred ceremony than the cheesy "what happens in Vegas, stays in Vegas" clichés. The minister's wife played the organ. Rather than the overused Elvis hits, she'd actually played classical music. Of course, it was a far cry from the hymns that would've been played in her father's church, but Shanice seemed okay with it.

Decked out in a white silk tea-length dress that looked enough like a wedding dress, Shanice sighed as if she were willing herself not to cry and said the words without reading them. "Trevor, even when we were children and you became my best friend, my protector, and my champion, I remember thinking that one day you would be my everything. You are the manifestation of what

God desired for me, even when I didn't know what to ask Him for. You loved me when I didn't know how to love myself. We've gone through some dark times, but as we join together today, I promise we only have to look forward to living in the light. I will love you until death parts us, and I can no longer say the words."

It was Trevor's turn, and he hoped his voice wouldn't shake. "Shanice, my heart is so full today, because it feels like we've always been joined together. Biological parents may have forsaken us, but we each were blessed with mothers and fathers who loved us more than blood, and they are with us in spirit today. When I look at you, I see the faith you've always had in me and realize only God could have put there. You have always been my friend, but as I take you as my wife and the future mother of my children, please know I will love you all the days I have on this earth and beyond, if possible."

The minster looked to Donald, "Do you have the rings?"

Donald did an elaborate patting of his pockets before he came up with the rings. Everyone took a collected sigh of relief when he grinned and held them out to the minister.

"Please repeat after me, Shanice. 'With this Ring I thee wed, with my body I thee worship, and with all my worldly goods I thee endow, in the name of the Father, and of the Son, and of the Holy Ghost.' "

Once they'd each repeated the only phrase they chose to keep from the traditional vows, the minister declared. "By the power vested in me by God, the State of Nevada, and the city of Las Vegas, I now pronounce you husband and wife. Trevor, you may kiss your bride.

The minister's wife began a rousing rendition of *Pachelbel's Canon in D* as Trevor kissed Shanice so thoroughly, her knees buckled.

"You two are married now, you don't have to keep making out like a couple of teenagers," Lisa said as she snapped several more shots of them in a lip lock.

"Yeah, last I checked your honeymoon suite was waiting for you on the strip," Donald said.

The minister said, "Mr. and Mrs. Kyle, we'd love to watch you two revel in your marital bliss, but I've got another couple getting married in ten minutes."

They finally pulled apart and joined hands before they walked quickly out of the chapel. Lisa, the minister's wife, and Donald threw rice at them as they exited.

Then they had dinner at a supper club, where they danced the night away. At one point, Trevor could see Donald and Lisa involved in a serious conversation. Lisa seemed to be on the attack, but Donald looked like he was holding his own.

Chapter Twenty Two

"I'm going to take things slow," Trevor said. "I don't want to hurt you."

Shanice nodded. "Okay."

As Trevor removed his clothes, he alternated by removing some of hers until they were both undressed. When they had their fill of looking at one another, he picked her up and carried her to the bed, where he laid her down. Shanice averted her eyes shyly and closed her legs.

He lay down next to her then leaned over and caressed her face. "I love you, Shanice. Don't ever forget that."

Trevor was more alive in this moment than he had ever been. He knew this wouldn't be the greatest lovemaking session of all time, but he'd try to make it special for her. He also had to make sure it wasn't over before it began. He first had to concentrate on making her relaxed and comfortable.

"Okay, just relax. Close your eyes." Shanice did as she was told. Then he brought his hand down and touched her. She jumped and opened her eyes. "It's okay. I'm just trying to get you ready." Shanice closed her eyes, and he began again. He slowly ran his finger up and down and could feel her getting wetter. This was good. That meant less pain for her. "How does that feel?"

"Mmmm...good," she said.

"Great. Now I'm going to slowly insert my finger. It may hurt a bit, but it'll help for what's to come."

Shanice nodded, and he carefully slid his finger inside her. She tensed for a moment then seemed to relax. He moved in and out of her and watched her face. She was so beautiful.

"Now I'm going to add another finger."

He hated to see the look of pain on her face, but it was about to get a lot worse. As he slowly worked his fingers in and out of her, the pain seemed to go away and turn to pleasure. Then she moaned and shook, and he felt her orgasm. It was the most beautiful thing he'd ever seen.

When she seemed to come down, he said, "Shanice, could you open your eyes and look at me?" When she did, he said, "Look, I've been in prison for seven years. I've been dreaming of this day for a long time, and now that it's finally here, I don't want to mess it up."

Shanice put her hand on his cheek. "You can't."

He smiled. "Well, we'll see about that. It's been a while. I'll try to hold on as long as I can, but this will probably go pretty fast. If it does, I'll make it up to you, I promise."

"Trevor," Shanice said, "no matter what happens, this will be amazing, because I'm with you. I've wanted this for a long time, too. We're going to be fine."

Trevor was relieved. This took a lot of the pressure off. He reached into the nightstand drawer and pulled out a condom from the pack he'd bought earlier that day. He was so nervous, his hands shook.

Shanice held out her hand. "I can do that for you, if you want."

Trevor almost came right there. At a loss for words, he just handed her the package. She ripped it open and slowly slid it onto him. This was the most erotic thing he'd ever seen.

He shifted on top of her, and they looked into each other's eyes. "I'm going to slide in slowly. If it gets to be too much, just tell me to stop, and I'll wait."

She nodded and looked as scared as he probably did. He guided himself into her and his eyes rolled back when he did. When he was able to focus on her beautiful face again, all he could think was how good she felt.

"Stop," she said with her eyes clenched shut.

Trevor froze.

Shanice breathed in and out a couple of times. "Okay," she said.

He went in deeper, and a couple of times he thought for sure she'd tell him to stop, but she didn't, until at last he was all the way inside her. He gave them both a few moments to get used to the sensation.

"Oh, Trevor," she said as she looked into his eyes.

He didn't think it was possible to feel more connected to Shanice than he already was, but the realization that this was really happening, after all the years of pushing her away and the trials with his uncle, made him nearly weep from joy. If everything he'd gone through meant he was leading up to this moment, he'd do it all again.

"I love you, Shanice."

"I love you, too."

He slid out, then in again, as he tried to keep his mind on anything other than what he was doing. It was difficult, but he wanted to make this good for Shanice. He wanted her to remember this. She wrapped her legs around him, which helped both of them. When he couldn't contain himself any more, he let go before he collapsed lightly on top of her and nestled his face in the crook of her neck. Then he proceeded to sob like a child.

Shanice comforted him until he composed himself. "I hope those were tears of joy and not grief that I was a lousy lay."

"You are insane," Trevor said as he sobbed a laugh and wiping away the remnants of his tears. "I was overcome by the idea of you waiting for me." He felt honored she had forsaken all other men to wait for him.

"You didn't think I was going to give it up to any old character, because you had a measly seven years in prison, did you?"

"College is a huge rite of passage. I couldn't be selfish enough to ask you to wait, but I'd hoped you would."

"Why did you never ask me if I'd had sex before?"

"I didn't want to know if you had, and I didn't have the right to ask you not to, considering how I'd pushed you away so much."

"I knew you never meant it."

"You had epic faith in me, baby, and I love you for it."

"*Have*," she said.

Chapter Twenty Three

"This hotel reminds me of growing up in Orlando," Shanice said. "It's so festive here."

"Yeah, the games are just little more adult-oriented," Trevor said and smiled. He stopped their slow promenade through the hotel lobby, cupped her face, and kissed her tenderly. "Present company is also much better."

Shanice beamed at him. "See, you're better at playing the doting husband than you thought you'd be."

"You make it easy," he said.

They reached the windowed foyer where the roller coaster was whisking by and riders were throwing up their hands in wild abandon, while others had a look of sheer terror on their faces. Shanice tugged on his arm. "Can we ride after lunch?"

"Yes. But we should give our food a chance to digest. We wouldn't want a *Sand Lot* moment happening on our honeymoon, now would we?"

"As long as we don't chew any tobacco after our meal, we should be good."

"You remember that much about that movie?"

She rolled her eyes playfully. "It was only your favorite movie of all time. You even layered your t-shirts with button-ups, just like Benny Rodriguez did."

"That was a brilliant fashion statement."

"Yeah, unique to you and millions of other boys who loved that movie."

They reached the restaurant and were seated.

"I'm starved," Shanice said.

Trevor laughed. "You're about the size of a gnat, girl. Where do you put it all?"

"In my compact little thunder thighs, and this round little tush you like so much," she said.

Trevor felt his face heat up. "Am I that obvious?"

She leaned in and planted a soft kiss on his neck. "Only to me." She patted his arm.

"I'll have you know, I love all of you. Never doubt that."

He was so wrapped up in the moment, Trevor almost forgot he needed to talk to Shanice about Philip. He hoped it would occur before they flew out to meet the Baileys on Friday. He didn't want Philip to know about his marriage to Shanice until Special Agent Hemphill and his team were able to get enough on Phillip to take him down, once and for all. They would have to construct an elaborate ruse, especially to keep Shanice safe. There was no time like the present to bring her in on things. Well, at least the things he could share with her at the moment. Some of what was going down would have to be on a "need to know basis."

"Babe?"

Shanice licked her lips in a way that made him want to run back to their room. "Yeah?"

Trevor mentally shook himself to clear all thoughts of a sexual nature from his mind. He had to be on his game. "Philip is likely to show up around here."

"Really? You mean now? While we're here?"

"Yeah. He wanted to pick me up from the facility, but I told him I'd made other plans. I'll be hooking up with him tonight or tomorrow." He said it fast, knowing she'd probably frown on him having anything further to do with his uncle.

"Trevor, do you really think that's wise? He's the reason you ended up in prison in the first place. Part of your rehabilitation is not having anything to do with the people you were in contact with before."

Trevor put his arm around her and pulled her close. "How do you know that?"

"Your caseworker told me."

"You became besties with my caseworker?"

"Stop trying to distract me."

"Okay, then. Will you trust that I'm not trying to go down that path again? I'm only doing this to prove something to the only people who matter to me. You and your parents. That's all I can tell you now, because keeping you away from Philip is the most important thing, and I need you to be as careful as possible moving around the city."

"Avoiding him won't be an issue for me. I never got the feeling he liked me very much."

"Philip doesn't like himself very much. You're right, though, he's nothing like David, believe me. The best decision I ever made was to keep you away from him after David and Elena died."

"Then why are you entertaining the idea of seeing him now, and on our honeymoon?"

Trevor had to be careful here. He didn't want to flat out lie to his bride. He would tell her the whole story some other time, when he was up for sharing just how pathetic his life had been with good old Uncle Philip.

"This is the best opportunity I'll ever get to take him down. If I don't do it now, while he thinks he has me at a disadvantage, it won't happen."

"David Kyle was a saint compared to his brother. Isn't it strange how two children who grew up in the same household can turn out so different?"

"Tell me about it. Hey, maybe you should stay at Lisa's the next couple of days, so you can be completely out of harm's way."

She was shaking her head before he was finished speaking. "No way. Trevor, we're on our honeymoon, and I'm not afraid of your uncle."

"Maybe you should be."

"And besides, you promised never to push me away again."

Trevor wished he'd qualified that promise more. "This is an entirely different situation, baby."

"Not on our honeymoon, it isn't."

He pulled her into his arms. "When did you become so stubborn? The little snaggle-toothed girl I remember used to always do what I said."

"She grew up," she replied and followed up with a kiss.

"Compromise," he said. "How about you stay at Lisa's just on the morning I'm working with the feds to catch Phil. We should have all that dirty business taken care of by noon."

"I think I can deal with that," she said.

He held his breath then blew it out and said, "Is your faith in me firmly intact?"

"Absolutely."

He leaned in and kissed his wife's delectable lips. "Good."

Chapter Twenty Four

The Las Vegas field office had an impressive array of computer gadgetry, the likes of which Trevor had never seen. What he'd done for the bureau while in the joint was small potatoes. With the equipment in this room, and a few other additions, Trevor could take down the computer systems of the entire world, if he were a "black hat hacker," which he wasn't.

Donald gave him a crooked grin. "This shit gives you a hard-on doesn't it?"

"In the worst way." Trevor grinned. "This is the closest my wife will ever come to identifying anything as my mistress."

"Good, because she and that hellcat friend of hers would make you a eunuch if you were ever to look sideways at another woman."

Trevor raised eyebrows with a look of incredulity. "Did Lisa threaten you?"

"And at your wedding reception, no less. She thinks I'm one of your criminal friends, and I'm a bad influence on you. She threatened to sic her 'high-ranking Air Force official father' on both of us. Shanice is his goddaughter, and she compared her father to a Corleone. That woman is fierce."

"And you like her." Trevor took a seat in front of a quad of computer monitors, touched the mouse, and the powerful computer woke up.

Agent Hemphill looked sheepish for the first time ever in their association. "After we bag your uncle Phil, I might have to reintroduce myself to Lisa Bradford, is all I'm saying."

Trevor laughed. Then he became immersed in the world of computer code. A world he understood better than any other, until he fell in love with one Shanice Anderson Bailey. Now it was time to protect her and her family from Philip Kyle's threats, once and for all.

First, Trevor pulled up the program he'd used to perpetrate his heist.

"See this string code right here?" Trevor said. "This is what I hid in the main code, so you guys could trace the program to me."

Donald pulled a chair next to Trevor and sat backwards in it then draped his hands over the back. "If you hadn't done that, we would never have caught you. Now that this is almost over, you want to tell me why?"

"When I went away to college, I thought I was so smart. I'd finally gotten away from Phillip and acted all cocky about it. Then the Baileys were in a car accident. Someone had run their van off the road when they were coming back from church. It's a good thing the children weren't in the car with them. Shanice had taken them to a matinee. Isaiah suffered a concussion and Brenda a broken arm. Afterward, Phillip let it 'slip' he might have been involved in that, too."

"He was sending you a message."

"Yep. At that point, I no longer asked 'how high' when Philip said jump. I'd severed my relationship with Shanice a couple of times, but he didn't buy it. Philip wanted me to know he wasn't bluffing about hurting the people I cared about most. It's the only way I agreed to do the unclaimed funds heist."

"Did you always have a plan to go to jail on his behalf? You could've rigged the code to frame him."

"Those goons he employed had mafia connections. His directive was if anything happened to him, they were to take out a hit on the Bailey family."

"So, you took the fall so he wouldn't use you to do his dirty work anymore?"

"Yeah, that and I knew it would take me several years to retrofit this program to catch Philip. I needed to go to jail to protect Shanice and her family and to buy the time I needed to write the new program."

"So, how is this going to work?"

"It'll go in reverse of the original program. I'll hack into the financial institutions around the world that hold the funds the original program took. We're talking institutions in all the places where the uber-rich hide their money, like the British Virgin Islands, the Bahamas, the Cayman Islands, Cook Islands, Belize, and Switzerland. There's several million in each location that when aggregated, is over a billion dollars, not to mention the interest that has accumulated. Philip believes his half of the code is required for me to access the money. That's true and not true. In six months, I was able to write a program to override his half of the code."

"You can do that in six months, but it took several years to override the original program?"

"I only had clearance to work on that when you brought me other projects to work on. The prison didn't give me carte blanche use of their computer systems."

"You mean you *took* clearance to work on it with my projects. Son of a bitch."

"My biological mother *was* sort of a bitch," Trevor said. "So I'm not offended by the term."

"Smart ass," Donald said. "So, once you come to work for us, you're going to teach me everything you know, right."

"Maybe not everything." He smirked. "It's called job security, my man."

"I'll settle for that. It'd be a far sight better than what the bureau currently has. You're the only hacker who's ever been able to completely cover their electronic footprint. I'd be happy to just know how to do that."

"Okay, we'll hammer out the details later." I'll be right back.

Trevor left and came back holding a toothbrush.

"What the fuck?" Donald said. "You about to brush the hell out of some ones and zeros?"

Trevor removed the handle of the toothbrush to reveal what looked like a USB connection. "This is how I stored the program I created while in prison. Two-hundred-sixty-four gigabytes of storage."

"In a goddamn toothbrush. Ingenious. The one item the prison would never have thought to take away from you or x-ray for contraband."

"True."

"But how did you get it inside?"

"If I tell you that, I'll have to kill ya."

"Funny guy."

Trevor took the USB and attached it to the computer. "Now, all I have to do is tweak this to send the money back to the original banks, rather than in the banks where it's being hidden. Philip will be none the wiser. All he'll see is that a huge sum of money has been transferred to what he believes are his off-shore accounts."

"Now, to go over what we'll need for an indictment," Donald said. "You have to get him to admit his part in the original crime."

"That shouldn't be difficult, given how much of a narcissist my uncle is."

"So, my men tell me Philip arrived today. He expects to have to drive to the prison tomorrow morning to meet you. Tonight might be a good time to make contact. Let him know what time you plan to meet up with him."

"Okay, here's hoping he has the same cell phone number."

"Oh, he does."

"I should've known you'd leave no stone unturned."

"That's why they pay me the big bucks."

"Yeah, yeah." Trevor turned his full attention back to his programming. "Now, to test this. Wouldn't want a bug to render this code useless or send over a billion dollars to places unknown."

"Right. That happens, we just might have to send you back to the slammer." Donald chuckled.

"Not funny, Agent Hemphill."

"Just kidding. I know you don't make those kinds of mistakes."

"Not if I can help it."

· · · · • • • • • • ● • • • • • • • • • · ·

Before he went back to the suite to join Shanice, Trevor called a number he'd never forgotten. Despite his uncle's penchant for dealing with him as if he hadn't used, threatened and blackmailed him most of his teenage life, Trevor's interactions with the man remained thinly veiled hostility. He was careful to maintain that tone when he called.

"Just letting you know, the feds sprung me early."

"Well, if it isn't my nephew the felon," Philip said. "My, how the wunderkind has fallen."

"Cut the crap, Uncle Philip. I'm only calling you because you're my next-of-kin on the books, and you need something from me."

"Oh yeah? Well, I'm already in Vegas. We were going to drive down tomorrow and pick you up, but since that's not necessary, the boys and I can make a later night of it on the strip. You want to hang with us?"

"Nah, I'm chilling with a honey I hooked up with since I've been out."

"Understandable, but you need to meet up with us first thing tomorrow. One full night of getting your dick wet for the first time in seven years should suffice."

"Yeah, you'll need to drop a bundle on some computer hardware if you want me to do that job first thing."

"Why can't we go back and do it in Orlando on the equipment I already have there?"

"That footprint has to be under surveillance, and I don't plan on going back to prison any time soon. If you want it done, it'll have to be done here, on a new system that I can rig so it can't be traced."

Philip was quiet for almost too long. "Okay, we'll get everything you need tomorrow, but we're keeping all the goddamn receipts, because that shit is going back right away."

"Sure thing."

Once Trevor hung up with Philip, he dialed Hemphill. "Those mafia guys are here with him for sure. He must owe their organization a lot of money, because they're not letting him out of their sight."

"I don't like the idea of you going in alone, Trevor. You need to create a plausible reason for me to be there. If he's entitled to two sidekicks, you should at least have one."

"Aw, Agent Hemphill, I didn't know you cared so much."

"I'm just saying, the bureau is invested in you now. It'd be a damned shame if anything were to happen to you. You've convinced me that Philip, or his muscle, could put a bullet in you the moment he gets the funds transferred over. He'll believe he has all the money."

"Fine, but I'm not calling him back tonight. You'll just go with me in the morning, and I'll explain the situation then. He doesn't like it, he can take a hike."

"Well, not really, because we still want to bag this asshole."

"Believe me, the element of surprise will be better. You just figure out how you're going to conceal a weapon. You'll be frisked."

"I'll put it where no self-respecting man will feel comfortable searching for it."

"Enough said."

"You're a wuss, Trevor. I'm going to have the bureau send you through FBI recruit training. You need to learn how to properly conceal and fire a weapon, if you're going to work with my team."

"If I wanted to do that, I'd have signed up for the military."

"Geeks like you don't usually like the military."

"That's where you're wrong. My Dad was a Marine and a bigger geek than I am."

"I stand corrected, then, but your ass is still running the obstacle course and learning to handle firearms. I insist on all my field and desk agents going through the same training."

"You don't think I'll be able to cut it, do you?"

"We'll certainly find out."

"I didn't veg in prison, man. You know I worked out religiously, and I can bench two-fifty."

"We'll see, computer geek."

"Goodnight, Donald. My bride is waiting on me. I don't have time to argue with you anymore."

"Meet you in the lobby at 0800 hours."

"Sharp." Trevor said and hung up.

Chapter Twenty Five

When Trevor walked into their suite, he could sense the tension in the air. Shanice seemed to be having a standoff with Lisa.

"What did Mom say?" Shanice said through clenched teeth. "Why didn't you just let the call go to voice mail? You let a little pastor's wife squeeze you—" Then she saw Trevor. "Hey baby. How'd your business with Donald go?" She smiled and ran to him as if it had been days since she'd seen him. She threw her arms around him and kissed him like there might be something serious behind it, but that would have to wait until later.

Trevor held her close for a few moments then looked into her eyes. "What's up with Isaiah and Brenda?"

Shanice's face fell. "I just need to remember never to share any state secrets with Lisa." Shanice stepped out of his embrace and folded her arms. She glared at her friend.

"Oops," Trevor said and turned to Lisa. "What did you do to piss my lovely wife off?"

Lisa frowned. She was wringing her hands together like a naughty child. "I might have told Mom and Pops Bailey you two got married."

"Ugh!" Shanice said. "Mom only has to hit her with the Claire Huxtable voice, and she sings like a canary."

"In my defense, you two never said *not* to tell them," Lisa said.

Shanice was nonplussed. "But did it not occur to you this news might best have come from Trevor and me?"

"Well, when you put it like that... "

Trevor stepped behind Shanice and pulled her back, then rested his chin on her head. "It'll be okay," Trevor said. "Isaiah and Brenda have always loved me."

"Until you told Shanice you never wanted to see her," Lisa said.

It was as if she'd dropped a bomb in the room. Shanice went still in his arms, and Trevor's mouth fell open. He turned Shanice gently to face him. "Is that true, baby?"

"Could be," Shanice mumbled.

Trevor rubbed a rough hand over his face and into his hair. "Well, that complicates things. A little. But if Isaiah and Brenda are anything like the people I remember, they can be reasoned with."

Shanice laughed. "Yeah. When have you known Mom and Dad to hold a really long grudge?"

"Never. We'll just fly home like we planned and ask him to marry us at his church a few Sundays from now."

"And we'll explain to him how we didn't want to wait another minute to be married—"

"Well, I could have waited, if you weren't so impatient about certain things."

"You did not just say that?" Lisa said then sat down on the sofa and grabbed a bowl of popcorn.

Shanice pulled away from him and held her hands up as if to warn him off. "It was your idea."

"It was the only way, since you were 'about to explode.' What was I supposed to do? I was willing to marry you the right way."

"Foot, meet Trevor's mouth," Lisa said.

Shanice stormed out. Then the bedroom door slammed. When Trevor tried to follow, he heard the lock click into place just as he put his hand on the knob. He pushed his hair back and turned back around to look helplessly at Lisa.

"Two days, and you're already in the dog house, bro," Lisa said.

"But it's the truth. Why is she so mad at me for speaking the truth?"

She put the popcorn down and patted the couch cushion beside her. "Come here, Trevor."

He walked slowly over to the sofa and sat down.

"You've lived in an unnatural environment for the past seven years, so you've got a little bit to learn about women, okay?"

"Okay. I'll do anything to make this right. Just tell me what to do."

Lisa turned off the muted television and picked up her wine glass then angled so she could speak directly to Trevor.

"Number one. Never ever, ever, ever tell a woman, especially one who is your wife, that a bad decision was her idea. Once you've sanctioned it, it's *our* decision, okay?"

Trevor nodded.

"Number two. Never have a discussion like that in front of friends. You guys are one now, and you need to project a united front. Got it?"

"See? I'm not ready to be a husband. Don't they have counseling for this sort of thing?"

"Yeah they do, and if I were you, I'd ask Pastor Bailey to give you guys the remedial version as soon as you get home. My advice is to shut the fuck up until then."

"I'll certainly try. Now, how do I get her to come out or let me in there?"

"You're on your own with that one."

"C'mon Lisa, you know Shanice better than anyone."

"This is true," she said and tapped her chin thoughtfully with her forefinger. "Okay, first I'd suggest a lot of groveling. I'm saying you need to be as repentant as you can. Then you need to give her flowers, *Godiva* chocolates, and make sweet love to her like there's no tomorrow."

"I can do all that." He stood and pulled his wallet out of his jeans pocket. "Hey, will you get the flowers and chocolate for me while I begin the groveling?" He handed her a hundred-dollar bill.

Lisa put the bill in her pocket and rubbed her fingers together. "Man, you've been in the pen too long. I'm gonna need at least another Benjamin to get the best for my girl."

Trevor gave her another hundred, which Lisa slid into that same pocket as she grabbed her purse and cell. "I'm off on operation 'get my bride back.' See you in a half an hour."

Trevor waved her off then meandered over to the door and knocked. "Shanice... "

Chapter Twenty Six

Shanice popped a truffle into her mouth then sniffed the roses sitting in front of them. "They're beautiful," she said. She looked into his eyes. "This is like a precedent, you know. Your next grand gesture will have to top this at least three-fold."

"I didn't mean to hurt your feelings by saying what I did. It was stupid of me. I'm so sorry." Trevor leaned in and ran his lips lightly over her cheek while he took in her scent.

They were cut from the same cloth, and feeling too exposed sometimes made them both disappear within themselves for a while. Fear of giving so much and not knowing if that person would be around when you really needed them, spooked people like them.

Brenda once told him that the more he pulled away, the more tenacious Shanice became. It was true. And not just with Trevor but with everyone she loved. Their biological mothers had loved them, he supposed, but they loved drugs more. Shanice didn't want to love anything more than the important people in her life, and he knew this about her. He needed to follow her lead, and as Lisa said, shut the fuck sometimes, so he wouldn't hurt her again like he'd been doing for years.

Trevor kissed his bride again, thrilled he could affect Shanice in a way he'd dreamed about for so long, without guilt or shame. He stripped his shirt over his head and flung it aside then he grabbed Shanice and kissed her again. She pulled away, took a few steps back, and frantically removed her own top before she beckoned him with her sexiest "come hither" look.

He reached around and unclasped the lacy pink bra she wore and pulled it forward. He bent his head and took a nipple into his mouth before freeing the bra from her arms.

Trevor still couldn't believe he was a free man, a married man, who could make love to his wife whenever he wanted. He was excited and nervous, even though she'd already given him the gift of her virginity. Wild-oat-sowing-in-college notwithstanding, he still worried he might not be any good.

He buried his fingers in her long, silky hair. The drapes were closed, but ambient light seeped under them, and he could see Shanice's perfect curves. He slid her shorts and panties down over her thighs and dropped them to the floor. She stepped out of them and stood naked before him. Her silhouette was amazing.

He stripped off his jeans and boxers and stood naked before her. The sight of each other kept them both in thrall for a moment. Then he walked her backwards toward the bed, their legs moving in tandem as if they were dancing, until they fell back onto it. They bounced gently then settled there, lips still locked.

Shanice reached her fingers between their bodies and brushed her nails lightly against him. He twitched with anticipation as his thigh muscles flexed. The taste of her lips and warmth of her body was reassuring, and his nervousness fled. In its place was the excitement of feeling her naked perfection against his body. They rolled on the bed until they were farther onto it with Shanice on top.

She scooted down and left a trail of kisses on his chest. Then she cupped him in her hand. Trevor shuddered and moaned when she slowly slid her hand back and forth. Then he switched their positions and crawled on top of her. He kissed her tenderly and slowly at first, before his desire worked him into a frenzy. He left a trail of kisses on her neck and traveled down her bare chest.

He moved up to face her again and kissed her lips as he positioned himself. She gasped when he entered her. As he began to move inside her, she dug her nails into his back.

The same bliss that had overtaken him the first time they made love came back again. It was as if he might burst into tears for the second time, because it felt so good, and he loved her so much. He forced himself to relax, to connect with her so completely that all he could express was joy. Soon, she fell into rhythm with him and rolled her hips along with his. They were both moving together as one, as they should be.

Perspiration dotted their skin, and he hoped they wouldn't slide out of their lover's embrace. Trevor could feel himself nearing a spectacular release, but he wanted Shanice to get there first, especially after last time. He leaned down and took one of her nipples into her mouth. That's all it took.

She gripped his hair, and he went deeper. Shanice threw her head back and rose to meet him. She said his name as she came, which caused him to lose control and thrust faster. Then his muscles tensed, and his entire body grew rigid before he let go.

"Oh, God, Shanice!"

He came in a brilliant wave of pleasure that surged around him and awakened each and every nerve ending. When the waves subsided, he pulled out and rolled over onto his back. He took her into his arms.

"I love you, Mrs. Kyle."

"And I love you, Mr. Kyle."

Trevor grinned and held her tighter, and she reciprocated. They lay quiet for several minutes until their breathing evened out. He dipped his head and kissed her. It was a deep, lingering kiss he hoped conveyed the words he couldn't speak.

He lay there holding Shanice until their syncopated heartbeats slowed to resting. Trevor had no idea what tomorrow would bring for them, other than getting Philip Kyle out of their lives for good. He didn't dare think beyond that to the confrontation with her parents, but he was now sure their getting married had been the right thing to do. Their lovemaking was proof of that, and he would never doubt again.

At last he snuggled her comfortably in the crook of his arm and closed his eyes. The last thing he thought before he drifted off was whether he could refrain from punching Phil's lights out when he saw him for the first time in seven years.

Chapter Twenty Seven

It didn't take Trevor long to remember another reason he hated doing anything programming-related for his uncle. The bastard stood looking over his shoulder half the time, as if he could understand what the fuck was going on. His stinky breath smelled of whatever the hell he'd eaten that morning, with whatever the hell he drank the night before oozing out of his pores.

"How long is this gonna take?" Phil asked anxiously as he looked at the Rolex stretched taut on his fat wrist. Time had not been good to Phil. No longer was he tall and muscular like David had been. He was just big and round. Drinking and eating junk food didn't contribute to a healthy body.

Hemphill looked up briefly from the computer he was manning, as if he was also interested in Trevor's answer. It was already half past noon, and Trevor had told Shanice they'd be done a half an hour ago.

"Once we get the code strung together, the actual transfer won't take long at all," Trevor said.

Phil put a thick hand on Trevor's shoulder. "Good, because we have a flight out at 3:30."

Trevor stretched as if he was trying to loosen up his muscles from being in one place for so long, but he was really shaking his uncle's hand off his shoulder.

"Why don't you have your lackeys call for some room service?" Trevor said. "It's going to be a minute." The knock from room service would be the cue for Hemphill's agents to storm the room.

His uncle looked at Frick, the nickname Trevor had given the shorter of the two hoods, and nodded. The little guy reminded Trevor of a Chihuahua. Frick picked up the phone.

"So, Trevor," Hemphill said. "How'd you come up with this idea? You never told me when we were in the joint."

"I wish I could say it was my idea," Trevor said. "But that distinction belongs to a better man."

Being the narcissist he was, Trevor was sure Phil wouldn't let an opportunity go by to toot his own horn. He was right.

"My nephew has an extraordinary skill, but he's a drone, a worker bee. I am the mastermind behind this project. You see, I once worked as a CPA for one of the banks that held unclaimed funds for the state of Florida. I kept looking at the balance growing daily, until one day I thought, 'I need to get me a piece of that.' I didn't know how to do all the fancy, schmancy programming to make it happen, but I knew a kid who could.

"Straight shooter my brother was, I knew he'd never help me, so I had to get him out of the way to have access to the kid. Next thing you know, my brother dies in a goddamn car accident, and I volunteer to get custody of his computer genius kid. All it took was a few video games, some top-of-the-line computer equipment, and I had the little fucker eating out of my hand. I took the idea for this heist to the Boss and he bankrolled the project until the piss ant got caught."

"Where is the Boss anyway?" Trevor asked nonchalantly. "I thought he'd be around to get his cut."

"He had urgent business in Miami," Phil said. "But don't you worry, he'll know the minute he gets his share. Speaking of which, I hope you don't think your buddy here is getting any part of our share. You're going to have to divvy yours up with him"

"Not a problem," Trevor said, never looking up. His innocent question had successfully given the feds the whereabouts of the mob boss.

Phil droned on and on, digging his own grave deeper and deeper, not knowing the room was bugged. Trevor and Hemphill continued to write a dummy program they would keep going until the knock came. Then Trevor would run the real program while Frick or Frack went to answer the door. They were in Hemphill's room, which Trevor pretended was his, while Shanice was safe at Lisa's.

This solved the problem of Hemphill carrying a gun on him. He just hid it in the room, along with anything else that could blow his cover. He also had a sniper in the building adjacent to them, ready to help if it came to a gun fight.

Room service knocked at the door twenty minutes later.

"Wow, they're fast," Hemphill said, which was the password to get his team ready.

Three things happened at once. Trevor started the program. Frack went to answer the door, and Hemphill retrieved his hidden weapon.

"Paydirt," Trevor said, and the digital counter began. He pointed to the screen to keep his uncle and Frick occupied.

"There's nothing more beautiful than watching the numbers populate as you become rich!" Phil said. A red dot from a sniper site appeared on Frick's head. Then within seconds, all hell broke loose.

When Frack opened the door, Hemphill drew his weapon. "FBI! On your knees, Philip Kyle! Hands behind your head."

Instead of agents rushing in, there was a surprised Pastor Isaiah Bailey, Brenda, and Shanice.

Frack saw his opportunity and rushed them, gun drawn, and pulled Shanice in front of him as a shield. Cold fury filled Trevor, but he shoved it aside. He rushed toward Frack and Shanice, screaming, "Let her go, goddamn it!" But Donald pulled him back. "Get down, Trevor!" Frack froze but didn't release Shanice, who was scared speechless, her eyes wide with fear. When Donald pulled Trevor down, a red dot appeared on Frack's forehead, and a second later, he dropped and took Shanice with him.

Trevor rushed over just in time to help Shanice push Frack off her. He felt over her body to make sure she didn't have any wounds, because blood and brain matter was all over her. There was so much blood, he was terrified for a second she'd been hit.

"Are you okay?" Trevor said, still examining her. "Are you okay?"

She was shaking so hard, there was no wonder she couldn't answer, but he needed to hear it from her. "Are you okay, baby, please?"

"Yes, yes." Then tears spilled from her eyes, and Trevor felt as if a hot knife had sliced into his gut. He wrapped his arms around her trembling body to hold her close while she sobbed into his neck.

When Trevor looked back, Donald had cuffed Phil and was reading him his rights, as the other members of the team descended on the suite.

· · · · · · •••••● •••••• · · ·

The women were sleeping off the trauma. Pastor Isaiah Bailey was a lot of things, but he wasn't a coward. He recovered quickly and wanted answers. Trevor gave him a brief synopsis about Phil's reign of terror in his life.

"Trevor, son? Why didn't you tell us? Had we known what Philip was doing, we would have gone to the authorities and let them figure out how to get you out of that situation."

"Uncle Philip had David and Elena killed, hoping to get custody of me so he could pay off his mob gambling debt. He also threatened Shanice and your family multiple times. Brenda's accident was not a hit and run. I knew he wasn't bluffing when he said I would never see Shanice again if I didn't do what he said. "

"So that's why you broke her heart, multiple times?"

"Yes. I'd rather she have a broken heart than be in danger."

"I know as a pastor, I'm not supposed to hate, but you were so cruel to my little girl, that it took everything in my power not to. I should have known the bond you two had for all those years was too indelible to be broken. She always had faith in you, even when we didn't."

"I know, and I'm going to spend the rest of my life trying to match her faith with my own."

"You'd better, or I might have to step down, so I can kick your ass."

"Pastor Isaiah!"

"Ass is in the Bible, son. 'Samson smote the Philistines with the jawbone of an ass.'"

Trevor laughed. "I've always liked your loose interpretations of Scripture."

"So, does this mean you'll be coming to my church?"

"If Shanice is there, I'll be with her. And we'll want to participate in some of your marriage counseling sessions before we repeat our vows at your church."

"That's a good idea, but didn't you two put the cart before the horse with this Vegas speed wedding?"

Trevor remembered what Lisa said and took responsibility. "With all due respect, sir, Shanice and I had been apart for seven years. We didn't want to spend another minute without each other, and I didn't know what would go down with my Uncle Phil. If I'd died in that altercation, I wanted it to be with her as my wife. I remember what I promised you and Brenda the weekend she sneaked over to USF to see me. If I ever were to become your son-in-law, I would do it decently and in order."

Isaiah Bailey took a long look at Trevor. "I remember a time when Brenda and I wanted you to be our son, but David wanted you so badly, and I had a new church, a new daughter, and then the twins. Responsibilities that were going to keep me hopping already. We knew the Kyles would love you as much as we did."

"And they did. They were a tragic loss, but I guess on some level I didn't feel like I deserved what I had with the Kyles."

"That's the one issue David and I quarreled about. Getting you professional help. He thought his tough love and Elena's nurturing were all you needed."

"That sounds like my dad."

"I'd be honored if you'd give me that title now."

"Okay...Dad."

Isaiah, being the touchy feely guy he was, pulled Trevor into a bear hug. Just when it felt like it might become a little awkward, he looked over his father-in-law's shoulder to see Shanice.

"Group hug!" She squealed and ran over to enfold herself in their arms.

When they released each other, the pastor said, "I think I'll go join my wife in a nap before dinner." Then he sauntered out of the room.

Trevor took Shanice's hand and guided her over to the sofa. "Come sit down, it's been a rough day for all of us.

"I keep seeing that guy's head exploding." She shivered, and he pulled her closer to his side.

"I'm so sorry you had to witness all that," he said.

"I should've just told my dad to chill, but he was so ticked. He wanted to talk to you immediately. I figured we'd find you guys just cleaning up, and you'd be done with everything. I had no idea we were walking into the middle of it. I should be apologizing to you. We could've ruined everything..."

"But you didn't, and now it's all over."

"Good. So, you want to get my parents their own room tonight after dinner?"

"I don't know. I think I need to catch up with Isaiah and Brenda a little more, before we go back to Florida."

Shanice looked at him as if he'd grown two heads. "We're still on our honeymoon..."

He laughed. "Just kidding. We'll get them a room."

"When did your sense of humor get so twisted?"

"When you live with a sick bastard like Philip Kyle, then spend seven years in a federal prison, you need a sense of humor."

She frowned. "We'll both need therapy when we go back to Florida."

"Now there's something else we can do together."

"That's all good, but I can think of many things that are a lot more fun," she said with a sexy smirk.

"Such as?"

Shanice kissed him, putting everything she had into it. When they parted, Trevor reached onto the side table and picked up the phone. "Hello? I'd like to book another room, please."

A Note from Bev Elle

Thank you so much for reading Obsidian Faith. If you enjoyed it, please take a moment to leave at review at your favorite retailer.

If you're interested in my future new releases, please sign up for my newsletter, read my blog posts, and find me on social media.

—Bev Elle

http://eepurl.com/3PosH

www.bevelle.wordpress.com

facebook.com/bev.elle.5

goodreads.com/bevelle

https:/twitter.com/Bev_Elle

Upcoming Books From Bev Elle

The Parisian Assignation

Stephen has lived most of his life believing he was an unassuming Cranford, son of Anne, a housewife and Douglas, a local family practitioner. He has finished college, begun a career, and is engaged to a swimsuit model. What more could an All-American Boy ask for?

On his twenty-eighth birthday, Stephen learns he is the sole heir to the fortune of Étienne François Masson, the legendary philanthropist and CEO of Masson Enterprises. To claim his fortune, and guard it against a hostile takeover by his father's half-brother, he has to move to Paris to learn all the ins and outs of the empire his late father left him.

The company hires an assistant for him before he arrives, one who is fluent in both English and French, and is someone with whom he shares an intimate past—someone he'd sooner forget.

American born Nicole Parker has studied abroad since she was in grade school, and is an MBA and expert linguist. She is excellent at what she does, but for some reason she rubs Stephen Cranford, entirely the wrong way. Will this Parisian assignation prepare Stephen to be an international tycoon, or will his assistant drive him to distraction, in more ways than one?

Coming in 2015!

Excerpt from The Parisian Assignation

Chapter 1

Stephen Cranford tried not to dwell on the fact that within the hour, he would meet and have dinner with one of the richest women in the world. However, it was all he could do not to salivate over the mere size and complexity of her portfolio; it was the wet dream of any broker worth his salt.

He loosened his tie as he left the Loop where he worked as an Executive Commodities Broker and maneuvered through the remnants of rush hour traffic in downtown Chicago. He wove through stalled lanes and bottlenecks in the same manner he traded on the Market, anticipating openings and making aggressive moves to claim them.

After another brutal day watching commodities do things they hadn't done since the big one day drop in 2008, he was ready for a gourmet meal and an expensive bottle of wine. The Dow was down more than 2000 points. Fears about the European sovereign debt crisis and the crumbling U.S. economy dominated the marketplace.

These events created fluctuations in the Market much like the death of billionaire Étienne François Masson had done earlier in the year, but that had been a cakewalk compared to current conditions. However, for Stephen, Masson's death had ranked in the league of a catastrophic event. The business tycoon had been his idol while in college.

Stephen would forever remember his location and what he'd been doing when he heard the news about Masson six months prior. He had been home, making love to Darcy, his fiancée, when a news bulletin interrupted his favorite jazz station.

Darcy had flown into Chicago for a photo shoot and declared it, in her own words, "Sex Sunday." She stripped upon arrival and they had spent the day christening various pieces of furniture in his condo. The woman was nymphomaniacal in her love of sex; who was he to complain? They worked each other over whenever she was in town, and their sexual gymnastics usually held him until she breezed through town again, invariably on the weekends.

He had Darcy bent over the chaise in his bedroom. She had orgasmed once already, and he worked at a frenetic pace toward his payoff when the music was interrupted.

"Billionaire Étienne François Masson, a French businessman best known as chairman and CEO of the French conglomerate Masson Enterprises, the largest luxury-products company in the world, has died at the age of fifty-four in a skiing accident at his resort in the Swiss Alps. According to Forbes Magazine, Masson was the world's fourth and Europe's richest person, with a 2011 net worth of forty-five billion dollars..." the radio announcer droned on about Masson and his accomplishments in life.

Stephen slowed his stroke and barked out a surprised exclamation. "Fuck me!"

"That's what I'm trying to do," Darcy gritted out through her panting, as he fell out of sync with her. "Move your ass, Cranford."

He'd felt her clench around him as hard as she could, like a reprimand. He reclaimed his rhythm, and in minutes had elicited another orgasm from her and found his own release. They collapsed in a heap on the chaise.

"You love me, don't you, baby?" she'd whispered, eyes vacant, her mind contained. She didn't expect a serious answer to her question which, in truth, was why their relationship worked.

She expected pithy, meaningless answers and he didn't disappoint. "More than a bull market." His heart was as inaccessible as her mind.

Within a minute or so, Darcy had exhausted her threshold for the obligatory cuddling after sex. When she began to squirm, he'd let her go. It was as if their roles were reversed in that respect.

The irony wasn't completely lost on him that he felt stronger about the death of a man he didn't know than for his and Darcy's relationship.

As fiancées went, she was perfect for him. She could have been high maintenance, but she was a fucking anomaly if he'd ever seen one. Darcy Vale was a supermodel whose face graced the pages of the world's biggest fashion magazines, but she worked all the damn time, traveling every week. That left him often to his own devices, which suited him just fine.

His engagement was as much a decision to yield to the status quo as an arrangement of convenience. He was twenty-nine and figured if he were to tie himself to anyone by the time he entered his thirties, Darcy would be the highest caliber of trophy wife he could get. There was no real love there, but she was gorgeous, a tigress in bed, and someone he didn't have to romance. She was busy, as was he, and her approach to their relationship was as practical as his own.

It was an arrangement Stephen was sure even Masson would have appreciated.

Stephen had often drawn parallels between Masson's personal life and his own. The man had gone through women like *they* were a commodity. Stephen had done the same years ago when the girl he'd considered the love of his life cheated on him. What past event in Masson's life had made him the kind of man he was?

While fascinated by the news about Masson, Stephen didn't harbor any ill will toward him like some undoubtedly did upon his death. In fact, he had rather enjoyed delving into Masson's business and life while researching his case study. Now though, it would seem that the man who had everything had died alone. Stephen would make damn sure that wasn't him in fifty years.

With her physical needs sated, and appeased by their pseudo-emotional exchange, Darcy had dashed for the shower. Stephen lounged on the bed and fired up his ever-present MacBook. Surely there was information about Masson's death on the internet. If anything could be categorized as such, this was *breaking news,* and it would profoundly affect his job at the Flagler Group in the short term and change market conditions in the long term. Masson Enterprises used any number of commodities and by-products in the manufacture of their luxury goods. Ripples from Masson's death would be felt through Exchanges around the world. He'd quickly read the front pages of several ISPs and the financial e-zines to which he subscribed.

Bemused, Stephen realized that though he was saddened by Masson's death, he'd been excited about how he'd clean up in the aftermath, so much so that he considered joining Darcy in the shower for a celebratory round. He knew she would want dinner, and dancing at a club. There was always later, after the club, and Darcy with a few drinks in her was a whole other phenomenon.

The memory of that day six months ago had come flooding back when he received a phone call from Madame Delphine Masson's personal assistant, requesting a meeting.

Stephen was glad he wasn't still working on the trading floor, because his conversations with clients, juggling of portfolios, and doing a half-assed job manning his own monitors were all a blur. He was also fortunate he hadn't worked on any discretionary accounts. Stephen could handle his more savvy clients' speculations and hedges with his eyes closed, but the phone call had robbed him of his focus.

It was rare he left work early, but curiosity about Madame Delphine Masson's request to meet had overtaken him, and he'd called it a day after putting in only nine hours, a record low for him. It was just as well; he had worked himself into a frenzy trying to figure out why *he* was summoned. Stephen would go just to see what she wanted, and how she had acquired his name. He didn't have to get involved in her "matter of a grave personal nature," as her employee had indicated earlier while making the appointment with him. What could it hurt?

~v**PA**v~

It was busy as Stephen entered Ria, The Elysian Hotel's Michelin two-star restaurant, but Madame Masson would have stood out in any crowd. Her regal confidence outshone the elegant simplicity of her attire. Stephen would guess she was dressed in the best that Masson Enterprises' designers had to offer. She sat on a chaise in the vestibule, flanked by two suits—presumably bodyguards, judging by the intelligence-grade earpieces they wore. It would have been foolhardy for a woman of her net worth to be in a foreign city left unguarded. She appeared comfortable and undisturbed by the obvious interest of the other patrons who looked on, wondering who this woman was.

Recognition sparked in her eyes, as well as another emotion that Stephen couldn't identify. Then, her stare became direct and blatant, her assessment bordering on rude. She was still a beautiful woman despite her advanced age. She stood with a warm smile as Stephen approached, grasped both his hands and squeezed them.

"Étienne, I am so glad you could join me," she said in perfect, albeit accented, English. She pronounced his name exactly as if she might have spoken to her own son. Stephen didn't correct her. She'd lost her son in a tragic accident. The least he could do was allow her that one indulgence.

While doing his case study, he'd found that Étienne was the French version of Stephen, which meant "crowned." He and the Madame's Étienne shared a similarity in their names, but that was where the comparisons ended. Masson might have been crowned prince of a business empire, but Stephen had just begun to embrace his potential as a businessman.

"Your invitation evoked equal parts honor and curiosity, I must admit," Stephen said with his own earnest, yet nervous, smile.

Who wouldn't want to meet the mother of one of the most accomplished and admired businessmen in the world?

"Please forgive me, I have a hard time with the name Stephen," she said.

"It's quite all right," he assured her.

The hostess approached, rescuing Stephen from the awkward greeting. "I see your dinner guest has arrived, Madame Masson. Your dining room is ready. Right this way."

Stephen stood aside and allowed Madame Masson to go before him as they followed the hostess through the restaurant to a private dining room. The hostess seated them at a table for twelve, but it appeared they would be the only two dining. The bodyguards remained outside the door.

Stephen noticed Madame Masson staring again, but this time her eyes glistened with what looked to be unshed tears. He wanted to ask if she were okay, but she spoke before he could form the words.

"I'm sure you must be thinking that this meeting has come from out of—what is that baseball term you Americans use?"

"Left field?" Stephen supplied.

"Exactly... " her voice was husky with emotion."I cannot believe that I allowed my husband to deprive me of this joy."

Madame Masson spoke in ambiguities but seemed harmless enough, so he would humor her in whatever purpose she had in mind. He'd get a fabulous meal from the type of restaurant he only patronized when he tried to impress a woman.

Perhaps sensing his unease, Madame Masson offered her assurance. "I promise, Étienne, I may be advanced in my years, but I am in possession of all my faculties. We will come to the business of this meeting soon, but first, let us get to know one another, have a meal together and I will tell you why I have sought you out."

"I know it's after the fact, but my condolences on the passing of your son. He was brilliant, and the direction in which he moved the business was a true inspiration to me."

Her eyes misted, and she dabbed them with her napkin. "I wish my François would have had the opportunity to hear you say that."

Stephen felt like a cad for reminding her of her grief, but he wondered if they were speaking of the same man. "François?"

"Our family referred to my Étienne by his middle name," she explained.

"My apologies, Madame. I know his death must still be difficult for you. By today's standards, he was still a young man."

"*Oui.* A mother lives with the possibility that her child might precede her in death, but prays all the while that it will not be the case. I am thankful for the fifty-four wonderful years he was with me." She cleared her throat delicately and took a sip of water.

By the time they ordered, Stephen learned that Madame Masson had been born in Marseilles, and had met and married Nicholas François Masson when she was just seventeen. Nicholas had been fresh out of college and a lion ready to devour the world. His two companies and hers were the seeds that created the original conglomerate, but their son, François, was the mastermind behind Masson Enterprises as it existed today.

"What was your son really like?" Stephen asked as he tasted his first course, veal sweetbread *crosnes*. Madame Masson looked surprised, so he felt obliged to explain his interest. "I was somewhat of a huge fan in college. He was the subject of my graduate case study, but you can only get so much information from periodicals and the internet."

Madame Masson's eyes lit up in delight. "François was quite the precocious adolescent, but driven to achieve, and proved to be as shrewd a businessman as his father. He excelled in sports and was quite a passionate champion for the less fortunate. Later in life, he was branded as a fun-loving Casanova by the media, no matter how philanthropic and well-meaning he actually was. He lost someone very dear to him as a young man. I don't believe he ever got over her."

Stephen noted her discomfort and offered his empathy. "Things that happen in early relationships can definitely color a man's perspective."

"You speak as one who's lost in love? You're such a handsome young man, and quite charming. I can hardly believe that a young woman would be stupid enough to let you go." She took a sip of wine.

"Oh, you'd better believe it." Now it was his turn to be uncomfortable, so he changed the subject. "You have a daughter who heads one of the business groups, correct?"

"Yes, Nicoletta is Vice-President of the Wine and Spirits Business Group. The Lefevre Winery and French Hops Distillery was my dowry, so to speak. Nicoletta fell in love with the vineyards when she was in her teens. It's been her life's work. One of her sons has taken an interest in the business and will most likely succeed her."

"Has it always been so easy to get the younger generations to embrace the family business?"

Madame Masson laughed and lapsed into French. "*Non, mon cher...* ," then self-corrected. "My eldest granddaughter is married and has two young children and no head or desire for business. Thankfully, she married a young man who is a great provider. My grandson, Arnaud, who is about your age, used his trust fund to found a dot-com about five years ago." She rolled her eyes. "I do not see the appeal in managing a product that you cannot see, but he's doing well, so that should be all that matters, *n'est pas?*"

"Yes, it is." The waiter delivered their main course, and Stephen admired the dish Madame Masson had suggested for him. "So, how does the American offering of French cuisine compare to what you're accustomed to?"

Madame dabbed her mouth with her napkin and gave his question a bit of thought before she answered. "As a French restaurant on foreign soil, it is exceptional, but nothing compares to authentic French food prepared with love in one's own home."

"I feel exactly the same way about my mom's cooking. When I was away at Harvard and then Wharton, I missed it so much."

Her interest seemed piqued as he mentioned his mother. "What was it like for you growing up, Étienne?"

Stephen told her about growing up in Chicago, playing little league, polo, golf, and piano. Barely breaching the upper middle class, his parents were masters of living within their means. The only areas in which they'd splurged had been their children's educations, from elementary to post-secondary. They had all gone to private schools, which boasted the finest academic curriculums and extra-curricular activities available.

He swallowed a bite of sole. "I had a happy childhood as childhoods go. My parents always worked. My dad's a physician, and my mom taught Elementary School for a few years, until she realized she'd much rather write children's books so she could be home with her family. She was modestly successful at it, enough to gift each of us with trust funds when we came of age."

"Are your siblings as successful as you are?"

"Maybe moreso. My brother, Gavin, is a law partner in a relatively prestigious law firm here in town, married with two sons. My sister Elise, also married, has a son and daughter and manages the Arielle Chantilly boutique on the Magnificent Mile not far from this hotel."

"Ah, both great careers. Your sister has exquisite taste. Arielle Chantilly is one of our clothing lines." Madame Masson said with genuine interest.

"Yes, it was one of the lines added after I did my case study at Wharton."

"We acquired it about six years ago," she confirmed.

"My sister likes the changes that were made by your company."

"That's good to know." Madame Masson repositioned the napkin in her lap. "Are you not attached, Étienne? You didn't mention a significant other, or children. Only those of your siblings."

"As a matter of fact, I'm engaged to Darcy Vale, a model with whom you might be familiar. She's been on Masson Enterprises' payroll a time or two."

"Why, yes. She's been the face for our fragrance and jewelry lines. A beautiful girl that one, but she doesn't strike me as the type who would settle down, take care of a husband and have babies. But then, what do I know? I'm a septuagenarian, and this is the twenty-first century."

Stephen didn't know why, but that statement made him feel like he'd been scolded by his grandmother. In fact, Madame Masson reminded him of his dad's mother, grandma Kitty Cranford.

He indulged her with a smile. "Maybe we work because I'm not the type to settle down and be taken care of, and I like my nieces and nephews just fine, thank you very much." Stephen noted they'd been served a Lefevre Chardonnay, and held up his wine glass in a toast.

Madame Masson touched her glass with his and laughed a hearty laugh. "Touché."

Stephen did not refuse dessert. One thing about gourmet restaurants that he both loathed and loved was their serving sizes always left room for dessert.

"Now, to business," she said without ceremony. "I have a proposition

"I'm listening," he said with a smile. The excellent food and expensive wine had made him amenable. Besides, Madame Masson was a great hostess.

Madame Masson fixed her grey eyes on his. "I would like for you to come to the reading of my son's will in France next week. I believe I will be in a position to offer you an assignment in Paris that will begin the process of grooming you to replace François. I'd like to think that my Nicholas and François, were they alive, would approve of this move."

Stephen's jaw dropped. "I don't understand," he said. "I'm an Executive Commodities Broker, not a CEO."

"However, you have an undergraduate degree from Harvard and a Masters in Finance from Wharton. Not chopped liver by way of business degrees, as you Americans would say."

"Wait," he said, his brow furrowed. "Why would you want *me*, a virtual stranger, to attend the reading of your son's will and head up your company, for that matter?"

"Go talk to your mother and father, then come see me again," she said in a cryptic tone. "I'll be flying back to Paris on Sunday in the company jet. I'd like you to go with me. The will reading is next Wednesday. Once you've spoken with your parents, I hope you'll wish to communicate again. I'll let the desk know that you're expected."

Stephen fought hard not to frown in his increasing confusion. "Madame, I've been making decisions without my parents' blessing for a decade. Why is it so important for me to have their approval?"

"It's not their approval I'm asking you to seek as much as their disclosure."

He was slightly taken aback by her serious tone and smiled to soften his response. "So, my questions are to remain unanswered for now? That's hardly fair."

"What would not be fair is for me to tell you what only they have a right to. Go, talk to your parents, Étienne." There was a note of finality in her voice, and who was he to argue with a seventy-two-year-old billionaire?

Stephen couldn't wait to have that conversation with his parents. He was ready, if it would help him understand why Madame Masson had propositioned him to accept an assignment at Masson Enterprises. He let the top down on his car as he headed back to his condo, hoping the crisp Chicago night air would clear his head.

He'd heard the rumors after Masson passed away. The family was purported to have launched a search for a long lost heir to Étienne Masson's fortune—a love child he'd fathered by an American woman.

Fuck! Does Madame Masson think I'm the heir?

Surely not, he thought. He was Douglas and Anne's son. He had his mother's eyes and hair and was just as stubborn and meticulous as his father.

If he were Masson's biological son, his mother would have to have cheated on his father, because he was the youngest of the Cranford children. Anne Cranford didn't seem to be the type to cheat, but neither did someone else he'd known.

Stephen looked at his watch; it was ten o'clock and if he knew his parents, they weren't in bed yet. His dad was probably reading a medical journal while his mom was watching the news. He picked up his cell phone and hit their home number on speed dial. His mother answered.

"Mom?" Stephen called much as he had when he was a kid coming home to an afterschool snack; he half expected to hear the admonishment to get his homework done and practice piano before he went out to play.

He could hear the smile in his mother's voice. "Stephen, you've been too much of a stranger lately. I thought we were more important than that extremely expensive paper you peddle over at Flagler."

"You know you are. It's just—well—Darcy was in town over the weekend, and—"

"Enough said, son. You two don't get enough couple time. I don't know how you manage to keep a long distance relationship going, to tell you the truth."

"It's a challenge we're both up to, I guess. Hey, can I come by? I really need to talk to you and Dad about something."

Her voice was gentle. "You know you're always welcome to come home."

"Okay, see you in twenty minutes."

~vPAv~